BEAVER TOWERS

THE SERIES

*F*ar away, on a magical island, is a castle called
Beaver Towers. It was once the home of happy
beavers – until they were betrayed by magic. Magic
which called up evil creatures from the world of
shadows. The animals of the island send out a call for
help and Philip, an ordinary boy, finds himself drawn into
the struggle to save them from the powers of darkness.

There are four exciting books in the *Beaver Towers*
series. Here they are in reading order:

Beaver Towers
The Witch's Revenge
The Dangerous Journey
The Dark Dream

Nigel Hinton was
born in London. He has written
fifteen novels, including four prize-
winners, and a number of scripts for TV and
the cinema. He enjoys swimming, walking, films,
reading, watching football and listening to music,
especially 50s rock 'n' roll and Bob Dylan

Some other books by Nigel Hinton

THE FINDERS

For older readers

BUDDY
BUDDY'S SONG
BUDDY'S BLUES

COLLISION COURSE
OUT OF THE DARKNESS

NIGEL HINTON

THE DANGEROUS JOURNEY

THE THIRD BOOK IN THE BEAVER TOWERS SERIES

Illustrated by Anne Sharp

PUFFIN BOOKS

PUFFIN BOOKS

Published by the Penguin Group
Penguin Books Ltd, 80 Strand, London WC2R 0RL, England
Penguin Putnam Inc., 375 Hudson Street, New York, New York 10014, USA
Penguin Books Australia Ltd, 250 Camberwell Road, Camberwell, Victoria 3124, Australia
Penguin Books Canada Ltd, 10 Alcorn Avenue, Toronto, Ontario, Canada M4V 3B2
Penguin Books India (P) Ltd, 11 Community Centre, Panchsheel Park, New Delhi – 110 017, India
Penguin Books (NZ) Ltd, Cnr Rosedale and Airborne Roads, Albany, Auckland, New Zealand
Penguin Books (South Africa) (Pty) Ltd, 24 Sturdee Avenue, Rosebank 2196, South Africa

Penguin Books Ltd, Registered Offices: 80 Strand, London WC2R 0RL, England

www.penguin.com

First published as *Run to Beaver Towers* by Andersen Press Limited 1986
Published in Puffin Books 1997

027

Text copyright © Nigel Hinton, 1986
Illustrations copyright © Anne Sharp, 1997
All rights reserved

Set in 12/14 pt Monophoto Ehrhardt by Rowland Phototypesetting Ltd, Bury St Edmunds, Suffolk

Printed and bound in Great Britain by Clays Ltd, Elcograf S.p.A.

British Library Cataloguing in Publication Data
A CIP catalogue record for this book is available from the British Library

ISBN-13: 978-0-14-038388-1

www.greenpenguin.co.uk

MIX
Paper from
responsible sources
FSC
www.fsc.org FSC® C018179

Penguin Books is committed to a sustainable
future for our business, our readers and our planet.
This book is made from Forest Stewardship
Council™ certified paper.

For Rita

WELCOME TO BEAVER TOWERS

A WITCH, SOME FRIENDS, AND DANGER . . .

How would you like to be carried away on a kite? How would you feel if the kite took you over the mountains, over the sea and far, far away from your home? That's what happened to Philip in the story *Beaver Towers*.

He finally landed on an island and met a little beaver, Baby B, and his grandfather, Mr Edgar. The old beaver told Philip about the terrible witch, Oyin, who was capturing all the animals on the island and locking them up in the castle called Beaver Towers.

Philip soon became friends with the beavers and the other animals who were still free – Mrs Badger and three small hedgehogs. These three hedgehogs look after Doris, a rusty old car, and because their names are Mick, Ann and Nick everybody calls them the Mechanics. Philip decided to help the animals and, after many dangerous adventures, he defeated Oyin and sent her back to her horrible master, the Prince of Darkness.

You can imagine how angry Oyin was. And when Philip got home, Oyin came to his town to get her revenge. The story called *The Witch's Revenge* tells how Philip escaped to Beaver Towers and how Oyin followed him and tried to catch him. It was a very scary time for Philip but in the end he managed to destroy Oyin by a clever trick.

Now Philip is back home again and, because Oyin is dead, he thinks that all his adventures are over and that he is safe. But you can never be sure with magic – lots of strange things can happen. As you, and Philip, will soon find out.

CHAPTER ONE

Philip noticed that something funny was going on as soon as he got back from school. First of all there were three mousetraps just inside the front door. He had just stepped over them when his mother called, 'Mind the traps!'

'Why are they there?' he asked as he went into the front room

She swung round from her desk, took her glasses off and rubbed her eyes. 'Noises,' she said. 'Pitter-patter noises ever since I got home. It's driven me crazy. You know how scared I am of mice.'

The second thing was his bedroom. When he went upstairs to change out of his school things, he was surprised to find that his bed looked as if it hadn't been made. Yet he could remember making it – not very well, it's true, because he had been a bit late getting up – but he certainly hadn't left it in the mess it was now.

Then he saw his comics. Usually they were in a neat pile under his chair, but now they were all over the floor. And his dressing gown had fallen off its hook on the door. And one basketball shoe was on the window sill and the other was on a chair. And all the postcards on his table had fallen over. And his toy basket was open and everything was higgledy-piggledy. And the waste-paper basket was on its side, half under the bed. And the more he looked, the more he felt that everything was out of place.

His mum often said that his room looked as if a whirlwind had been through it and that's exactly how it looked now. But who could have done it? Megs? No. She sometimes knocked things over with her tail when she wagged it if she was excited or happy, but she couldn't have unmade the bed. Besides, she never came upstairs.

It was a mystery and Philip didn't like it. He felt suddenly all cold and goose pimply. It reminded him too much of . . . No, he mustn't think about that. He would only get frightened. Instead, he would whistle or sing and get on doing things to stop him from thinking. He hurried round the room, tidying things up, and then he got changed into his muck-around clothes – but no matter how hard he tried, he couldn't whistle or sing. It was silly really, but he preferred to keep quiet so that he would be able to hear any strange sounds.

He didn't feel properly relaxed until he ran down the stairs and into the front room. He sat in his favourite chair and Megs came in from the kitchen and put her head on his knee. He scratched and rubbed her ears the way she loved him to do and he chatted with his mum about things that had happened at school. About ten minutes later he decided to go out to the garage and do a bit more painting of his bike. He was really pleased with the bright yellow colour that he'd chosen.

He soon became so busy making sure that this third and final coat was perfect that he forgot all about the strange creepy feeling that something wasn't quite right. He didn't think about it during tea, either, or during the washing-up which he did on his own while his mum went upstairs to get changed for her evening class. But then something happened that sent the shivers up and down his spine again.

As his mum came downstairs, the door bell rang. It was Mrs Nelson. She had come to pick up his mum early for the class because she had to go across to the other side of town to fetch another lady whose car had broken down.

'You don't mind being left on your own, do you, Phil?' his mum asked. 'It'll only be for a couple of minutes. Your dad promised he'd be back at half past six and it's nearly that now.'

He wanted to say, 'Don't go. I hate being left alone in the house when it's dark. The last time

I was alone a witch called Oyin broke into the house. And when I got home today I noticed all kinds of strange things. No, please don't go.' But he didn't. After all, he was a big boy now, wasn't he?

'Course, I don't mind,' he said.

'That's my boy,' his mum said and gave him a kiss on the cheek.

The front door had hardly closed when the phone rang. Philip's heart thumped. Just like last time. Oyin had rung to check he was alone before she had come round to get him. But Oyin was dead. He had seen her skeleton in the sea. And even witches couldn't come back to life. Or could they? He picked up the phone.

'Hello, Phil. It's Dad here. Can I have a quick word with Mum?'

'She's just gone out.'

'Blast! I was supposed to get home before she left, but I've been held up in a meeting. It's very important and I'm going to be another hour, at least. Look, Phil, you don't mind, do you? You're old enough to look after yourself – not frightened of bogeymen and all that. What do you say? You'll be all right for an hour. Hmm?'

Philip gulped. 'OK. See you later then.'

'Yes. There's a good lad. I'll stop and buy you a treat – some chips or something. Bye.'

The phone clicked and his dad had gone. Too late to say anything. And while he'd been on the phone, he'd seen the lights of Mrs Nelson's car disappear down the road.

He was alone.

CHAPTER TWO

Philip sat down in the front room and tried to calm his pounding heart. Whatever he did, he mustn't think about things like witches and magic. But each time he told himself not to think about them, he only thought about them more. He could remember every detail of that terrible time when Oyin had come. Her dark figure across the street, watching the house. Her long, bony fingers coming in through the letter box and tap-tapping their way towards the lock. It had been horrible.

But he mustn't think about things like that. It would scare him to death. It was ridiculous. Here he was in his own home with all the doors locked. The lights were bright. There was a warm fire burning cheerfully in the grate and his lovable dog, Megs, was asleep in front of it. There was nothing to be scared of. He picked up a book and started to read. At first he had to force his eyes to follow the words but bit by bit he lost himself in the story.

Everything seemed still and peaceful when suddenly Megs opened her eyes and lifted her head. She had heard something.

Philip's heart started to thump again as he strained his ears. He held his breath and sat quite still but he couldn't hear a thing. Megs yawned and stretched then lay down again, put her head on her paws, and closed her eyes. It had been a false alarm.

Philip had just got back into the book when Megs sat up again. She cocked her head to the side and looked up towards the ceiling. And this time there was no doubt. She had heard something. Her tail beat twice on the floor, then she whined and got up and ran to the door. Now Philip heard it, too. A pitter-pattering noise from upstairs in his bedroom. Something was moving around up there.

Hardly daring to breathe, Philip tiptoed over to the door and opened it slightly. Megs whined again and tried to push her way past him.

'Ssh, girl. Good girl, stay here!' Philip whispered, holding on to her collar.

He leaned his head out into the hallway. There it was again, but louder now. A pitter-patter. That must have been what his mum had heard this afternoon. But it couldn't possibly be mice — it was much too loud.

What should he do? He could make a quick

dash to the front door and run outside into the road – but it was a dark, dark night out there, and perhaps those noises were just a trick to make him leave the house. No, much better to stay in here where it was nice and bright and the doors were safely locked. Except, of course, he wasn't sure what else was locked in the house with him.

Pitter-patter. Pitter-patter. Rustle. Rustle. There it was again.

Whatever was making those noises might be bigger than a mouse, but it certainly didn't sound loud enough to be a witch. On the other hand, witches could turn themselves into any shape they liked.

Perhaps the safest thing would be to close the door and stay in this room with Megs. He could push heavy things in front of the door and just wait until his dad came home. He could even open the window a little bit and jump outside if those pitter-patterings came down the stairs and some-one, or something, tried to come in here.

Yes, he could do that; but the trouble was that a voice inside him was telling him to go up the stairs and find out what was up there. If he stayed here, the voice was saying, he would only become more and more scared. It would be much better to go up and see what was really there. And, almost before he knew what he was doing, he had opened the door fully and was standing on the bottom step of the stairs.

Slowly, treading as softly as possible, he began to climb the stairs. Halfway up he turned and looked down the hall. Megs was standing at the bottom of the stairs. Her mouth was open and her tail was wagging in excitement. She obviously wanted to come with him but she had been trained never to go upstairs.

'Come on, girl!' he whispered and she wagged her tail even more and whined, but she didn't move. It was no good – he'd have to go alone.

Five more steps to go and he would be on the upstairs landing. Four. Three. Two. One. Creak! The top step creaked and groaned so loudly when he stood on it that he almost fell back in fright. He waited for a moment, looking at the half-open door of his bedroom, wondering if something might jump out towards him. It was dark in there, but nothing moved. He looked down the stairs – Megs was still there. Oh, if only she would come with him. He took a deep breath and walked towards his room.

He stopped at the door and leaned in to put on the light. The switch was quite a long way inside and he groped around, feeling that at any minute something might grab his arm. Then, click! he found it, and the light went on. He pushed the door open wide and looked in. Everything seemed normal. He took one step, then another, and he was in the room.

He glanced round. Nothing. Then he ducked

down and peered under the bed. Nothing. Could something be hiding on the other side of the drawers? He tiptoed forward. Nothing. The room was just as he had left it when he had tidied up.

Perhaps, after all, those noises had just been the sort of noises you can always hear in houses when it is quiet. He would go downstairs and put some music on or watch TV and forget about all these scares. And his dad would come home and he would be able to laugh about how silly he had been to be frightened. And yet . . . something wasn't right. There was no noise and no sign of anything, yet Philip had the feeling that he wasn't alone in the room.

There was one place he still hadn't looked. The wardrobe. Hadn't the wardrobe door been fully closed when he'd been up here last? He was sure it had. And yet now it was slightly open. Could there be something inside?

He walked forward and got hold of the handle. Don't wait – look inside. He pulled hard and as the door swung open something brown and furry leaped towards him.

Philip closed his eyes and stepped back. A weight hit him in the chest. Arms closed round his neck and he staggered and fell backwards on to the bed. He was just about to scream and scream for help when a warm tongue licked his face and a funny little voice shouted in his ear, 'Flipip!'

He opened his eyes and found himself looking into the face of his dearest friend, Baby B.

CHAPTER THREE

Baby B. The little beaver jumped off Philip's chest and started bouncing up and down on the bed.

'Flipip! Flipip!' he shouted. 'We comed all the way to finding you. And we done a magic spell and we whooshed and all of a sudden we was here. And it was a bit dark in the cupboard but I wasn't scared. And then we heared you coming up the stairs and you might be a monster but you wasn't. And . . .'

'Wait a minute,' Philip said, reaching out and pulling Baby B on to his lap, 'you're going too fast as usual. First of all – who's we?'

'Me and Nick, of course,' Baby B said, pointing to the cupboard.

Philip looked down. Just peeping out from behind a shoebox he could see a little pointed nose and two bright eyes.

'Nick!' he said softly, and the eyes blinked.

Then the shoebox jerked as the small hedgehog pushed his way out. He scuttled over the floor and tried to climb up Philip's leg but he fell off and rolled up into a tight ball. Philip bent down and gently lifted the prickly ball on to the bed. 'You're safe now,' he said, and the ball unrolled.

'Hello,' Nick said shyly and then giggled as Philip gave him a stroke on the tip of his nose.

'Now, Baby B,' Philip said, 'tell me as slowly as possible what all this is about.'

It was never much use asking Baby B to go slowly and he jumped up and started rattling away, hardly stopping for breath.

'Grandpa Edgar wants you to come to Beaver Towers. I know because he said to Mrs Badger and I was there and he said, "We need that young Flipip here, that's what we need – but how can we send for him?" And I sturgested to send the magic cloud and you could come on the dragon kite like before. But he said this time we couldn't doing it like that and we needed a messager who could go and tell you the message. And then me and Nick wanted to be the messager and Mrs Badger said it was too very dangerous. But Grandpa Edgar said it was the only way and it would be a good test for us.'

'What did he mean by that?' Philip asked, trying to slow Baby B down a bit.

'I don't know,' the little beaver said and then raced on. 'And then this morning – it was millions exciting, wasn't it, Nick? Grandpa Edgar taked us to the library and he said we had to be very brave and then he did the magic spells and then – WHOOOSH! – we whooshed, didn't we, Nick? And we held paws, didn't we? And when we stopped whooshing we was here. And we was looking for you but then this lady kept coming up the stairs and we hided under the bed and she banged her feet and said "Shoo! Shoo!"'

'That was my mum,' Philip said. 'She thought there were mice around and she's frightened of them.'

Nick giggled at the idea of being frightened by mice and then put his paw in front of his mouth in case Philip thought he was being rude. But the idea was so funny that he couldn't stop the giggles and he had to run across the bed and hide behind Baby B. This started Baby B off and soon the two of them were rolling around giggling helplessly.

Philip couldn't help smiling as he watched them – they were young and silly and funny and he was so pleased to see them – but some things were puzzling him. First of all, why did Mr Edgar want him to go back to Beaver Towers? Then, why had he sent these two little creatures on such a dangerous errand? And lastly, but most importantly of all, just how were they supposed to go back?

He waited until Baby B and Nick had nearly

stopped their giggles then he asked, 'Did Mr Edgar tell you what to do?'

'He said we should be brave,' Baby B said.

'And careful,' Nick added.

'Yes, but did he say anything about how we are all to get back to Beaver Towers?'

There was a silence as Baby B and Nick looked at each other, then shook their heads.

'I've got a good idea,' Baby B said at last. 'You can take us.'

'But how? The only way I know is flying on the dragon kite with the cloud but Mr Edgar says we can't do it like that.'

Baby B's eyes grew large and round and Nick's little mouth opened wide as they both began to realize what Philip was saying. Philip could see how they had both jumped at the chance of the adventure without thinking about the dangers and difficulties. But why had Mr Edgar let them come? Surely he wouldn't have done it unless there was a way for all of them to get back?

While Philip was wondering about this, Baby B and Nick came and sat quietly on his lap and held each other's paw for comfort. Then suddenly Nick stood up and whispered in Baby B's ear.

'Yes!' Baby B shouted. 'I forgetted all about it. Grandpa Edgar gave me a paper for you.' He reached into the top pocket of his dungarees and brought out a piece of paper.

Philip took it and unfolded it. He just had time

to see a strange drawing and to glimpse some words at the bottom when he heard a car stop outside his house. His dad was home!

'Quick, you two – into the cupboard. That's my dad and he mustn't see you,' he shouted as he stuffed the paper into his pocket.

Both the animals squeaked in fright. Baby B jumped up and grabbed Philip round the neck and Nick curled up into a ball. Unfortunately, Nick had forgotten how near he was to the edge of the bed and he rolled right over the side and dropped to the floor with a loud thump. At once he unrolled and started to run – straight out of the door.

'Quick,' Philip shouted, unhooking Baby B from round his neck and putting him on the floor. 'Catch Nick.'

Baby B went charging out of the room and Philip raced after him. He was just in time to see Baby B grab hold of Nick at the top of the stairs.

At the same moment, there were two noises – a loud growling from Megs, and the sound of the front door opening. Nick took one look down the stairs and bolted back towards the bedroom. He dashed past Philip and shot through the door.

Baby B was left standing at the top of the stairs. His mouth was open and he was so frozen with fear that he didn't even move when Megs growled again. Philip walked to the top of the stairs and saw his father and Megs standing at the bottom. They were both staring up at Baby B.

CHAPTER FOUR

'What on earth is that?' Philip's father asked, pointing up the stairs at Baby B.

'Oh, hello, Dad,' Philip said, as calmly as he could, and then bent down and picked up Baby B. 'Don't move,' he whispered into the little beaver's ear as he stood up again. Then he said out loud, 'It's a sort of teddy bear.'

'A what?' his father said.

'A sort of teddy bear. I found it at the bottom of my toy basket. I'd forgotten all about it. It's nice, isn't it?' Philip said and stroked Baby B's head, hoping he would have the sense to keep still. 'I haven't played with it for years but it's ever so lifelike, isn't it? You can even make it stand up. I left it at the top of the stairs to tease Megs.'

'Yes, well . . . You're a bit old for teddy bears, aren't you?' his dad said, looking away and taking his coat off. Philip seized his chance and dodged back to his bedroom.

'Don't you want your chips?' his dad called.

'Just coming,' he shouted back.

Nick was rolled up into a ball next to the cupboard. Philip put Baby B down behind the shoeboxes then nudged the hedgehog in alongside him.

'Now, just stay there, you two, and don't move. I'll be back up presently,' he whispered.

'Flipip,' Baby B said in a tiny voice.

'Yes?'

'Will that growler come upstairs and eat us?'

'That's not a growler, silly,' Philip said gently. 'That's Megs, my dog – she wouldn't hurt a fly.'

'But I isn't a fly – and she might hurt me,' Baby B said.

'Don't worry. I'll close the cupboard door *and* the bedroom door, then you'll be quite safe. All right?'

Baby B nodded, so Philip closed the two doors and ran down to the kitchen.

He sat down to eat his chips but somehow, after all the excitement, he wasn't very hungry. His dad was too busy reading his paper to notice, though, and Philip managed to slip most of them under the table to Megs. When they were all gone, he just wanted to go upstairs to his room but he thought his dad might get suspicious if he looked too keen to go to bed so he sat in a chair and tried to read. The time seemed to creep by but at last his dad looked up and said, 'Hey, off to bed with you.'

'Oh, Dad,' he said, as if he wished he could stay up.

'No arguing, Phil. I've let you stay up later than usual.'

'OK. Night, Dad.'

'Night, Phil.'

He tore upstairs but when he opened the cupboard door Baby B and Nick were curled up together, fast asleep. He had wanted to talk to them about things but they were probably very tired so he closed the door quietly. As a matter of fact he was feeling a bit sleepy too. By the time he had undressed and brushed his teeth he could hardly keep his eyes open. He slipped into bed, turned off the light and, almost before his head touched the pillow, he was asleep.

When he woke, it was still pitch dark but someone was rocking his shoulder like his mum did in the morning.

'Who's that?'

'It's me, Flipip,' Baby B said. 'Me and Nick waked up and it's a bit ever so dark and lonely in the cupboard and Nick says he is scared . . .'

'I didn't!' Nick said in the blackness. 'It was you what said it was scaring and we could go in Flipip's bed.'

'It wasn't!'

'Yes, it was!'

'Ssh! You'll wake everyone,' Philip whispered and then raised the edge of his bedcovers. 'Come on then, slip in here – but no talking, all right?'

Baby B lifted Nick in and then climbed in himself. There was a slight prickle on Philip's leg as Nick moved under the covers and settled himself down right at the foot of the bed. Philip felt Baby B's warm, furry body snuggle up against him and in no time at all he sank back into sleep.

CHAPTER FIVE

Philip had meant to wake up early to make sure that Baby B and Nick were safely hidden when his mum came in, but he overslept. From far away he heard the swish of the curtains and then the voice of his mum calling him.

He was wide awake at once, with his heart pounding fast. He blinked in the bright sunlight and sat up. His mum was staring at the two lumps in the bed next to him.

'Honestly, Phil, I really do think you're a bit old to be taking teddies to bed with you. Your dad said he found you carrying one about last night. What on earth has come over you?'

'Nothing. It was just a laugh.'

'Well, I don't think it's very funny. Anyway, hurry up – it's gone half past seven.'

As soon as she had gone, he jumped out of bed

and pulled back the covers. Baby B and Nick were still curled up asleep.

'Come on, you two,' he whispered and shook them. They opened their eyes, yawned and then both jumped up as they realized where they were. 'Ssh!' Philip warned, before they had a chance to speak. 'You must both go into the cupboard and be very, very quiet.'

He hid them behind the boxes again then rushed to get washed and dressed. When he got downstairs his dad had already gone to work. His mum was so busy that she didn't notice him slip two pieces of buttered toast into his pocket. He also managed to slide an apple up his jumper and when he finished his breakfast he dashed upstairs to give the food to his two friends.

'Now, listen carefully,' he said to them as they started to eat. 'I've got to go to school. When I get back we can decide what we're going to do.'

'We can do a good plan and you can be the organdizer,' Baby B said, with his mouth full of toast.

'And we can all go whooshing home, won't we?' Nick asked.

'I hope so,' Philip said, 'but meanwhile I don't think it's safe for you to stay in my room and I've thought of a really good place to hide. I want you to wait until everybody has gone and the house is quiet. Then you can creep downstairs, go out of the back door and hide in the shed at the bottom of the garden. No one ever looks in there so you'll be safe. All right?'

Baby B and Nick nodded and went on munching the food happily. Just at that moment his mum called to say he was late. Philip grabbed his school things, said a quick goodbye and ran downstairs. His mum handed him his sandwiches, gave him a quick kiss on the cheek, and bundled him out of the front door.

It wasn't until he got to school that he had a terrible thought that made his heart jump – what about Megs? He had forgotten all about her. What would she do if she saw a beaver and a hedgehog come down the stairs?

There was nothing he could do except cross his fingers and hope. All day long he imagined awful things – supposing Megs got scared or angry and bit Baby B or Nick? He tried not to think like that, but he couldn't stop and a couple of times his teacher told him off for not keeping his mind on his work.

At the end of school he ran all the way home. He burst into the kitchen so fast that his mum jumped in fright.

'Oh, don't do that!' she said. 'I've had enough excitement for one day.'

Philip knew something terrible had happened. His legs suddenly went weak and his mouth went dry so that he couldn't speak. But there was no need to ask questions – his mum couldn't wait to tell him.

'You'll never guess what I found in here this morning. A hedgehog and a beaver! Just imagine. And that's not the end of it – the beaver was wearing little dungarees. I was out in the garden hanging up the washing before going to work and suddenly there was all this barking and growling from Megs. And when I came in, there she was standing next to the fridge with these two animals crouching in the corner. They must have run in while the door was open. Goodness knows where they came from. The vet said they might have escaped from a circus.'

'The vet?' Philip managed to say, though he felt so weak that he had to lean against the table for support.

'Yes, I called the one near your school to come and take them away. I didn't know what else to do.'

'And did he?'

'What?'

'Take them away?'

'Yes, thank goodness. I hope he doesn't have to put them to sleep, though – I would hate that. I know it sounds silly but they looked really sad when he put them in a box.'

Philip's eyes filled with tears. 'Didn't they say anything?' he asked. It was only when he saw the funny look that his mum gave him that he realized what he'd said. 'I mean didn't *he* say anything? About what he was going to do?'

His mum started talking again but Philip couldn't listen. Poor Baby B and Nick. They must have been so scared when they bumped straight into Megs. A tear trembled at the edge of his eye and then spilled down his cheek. He turned away and wiped it quickly so his mum didn't see. Crying was no good – it wouldn't help Baby B and Nick. He must do something. Somehow, he had to go and rescue them.

He waited until his mum finished telling her story then he asked if he could go round and see one of his friends. His mum said yes but that he had to get out of his school things first.

Philip rushed upstairs and changed as quickly as he could. He took some money out of his savings tin and left the house without even saying goodbye.

CHAPTER SIX

Philip stood outside the vet's surgery for a few minutes trying to think of a good story he could tell him. But in the end he couldn't think of anything so he just opened the door and went in.

'Yes?' said the girl behind the desk.

'Um . . . I've come to get Baby B and Nick,' he burst out.

'Who?'

'My beahog and hedger,' he said, getting all hot and confused. 'I mean, my hedgehog and beaver. They ran away from my house and the lady across the street found them and the vet came and . . .'

'Oh, they're yours, are they? Hold on a minute.'

She got up and went through a door into the back of the building. Philip could hardly believe his luck. It was going to be easy.

Unfortunately, it wasn't at all easy. The door opened, but it wasn't the girl, it was a man in a white coat. He was short and fat and he was wearing very thick glasses that glinted in the light so you couldn't see his eyes.

'Come!' he ordered in a very unfriendly voice and marched off down the corridor.

As soon as he went through the door, Philip noticed a horrible smell of chemicals and when he caught up with the man he saw that there was a small spot of blood on the back of his coat. At the bottom of the corridor the man opened a door. He flicked a switch and a dim light came on to show a large, cold room filled with rows of cages. Philip glanced at them but they all seemed empty. Then, at the far end of the room, under a dirty window, he saw a couple of shapes in a larger cage.

'Over here,' the man said, and led the way to the cage. As they got near, Philip could see Baby B and Nick stand up to see who was coming. He had an awful feeling that he knew exactly what would happen next, but there was nothing he could do to stop it.

And sure enough, as soon as Baby B saw who it was, he leaped into the air and shouted, 'Hooray, it's Flipip.'

The vet stopped in his tracks and his mouth fell open in shock. He peered at the cage then looked round to see if there was anyone else in the room.

'Did . . . did you hear that?' he said in a scared, squeaky voice.

'What?' Philip said, as calmly as he could.

'That!' he pointed a trembling finger at the cage. 'That beaver said "Hooray" or something.'

'I didn't hear anything,' Philip said. Then he added, in case Baby B hadn't realized, 'Beavers can't talk, can they?'

'No, no – of course they can't,' the man said, as if he was trying to convince himself. 'No, of course, beavers can't talk but . . .' he peered closer, 'there's something funny about this one. When I was bringing them back in my car, I kept hearing things as if someone was whispering.'

Philip looked at him as if he couldn't understand what he was talking about and the vet coughed and changed the subject. 'Anyway, they're definitely yours, are they?'

Philip nodded.

'Well, you'd better go home and get your parents to come and pick them up. I can't hand them over to you. I need an adult to sign the form.'

'Oh no!' Baby B said. And this time both Philip and the man jumped in surprise.

'Oh no, oh no!' Philip said quickly, trying to cover up.

The vet scratched his head and looked at the cage and then looked at Philip. 'Was that you, or was that . . . ?'

'I just said "Oh no!" because my parents are out and I won't be able to get them to come this evening. Can't you let me have them? I've got some money to pay for them. My parents can sign the thing tomorrow.'

'Sorry, can't be done. All animals must be signed for. Now, off you go.' And before Philip could argue, the man started pushing past the cages and out of the room. As the door closed, there were two small, sad cries of 'Flipip!' but luckily the man didn't hear.

As soon as he got outside, Philip ran along the row of shops until he came to the alleyway that led to the rear of the buildings. He soon found the vet's house and began to wipe the dirt off the window so that he could peer into the room. There, just below him, was the cage with Baby B and Nick huddled together, crying. He tapped on the glass and they looked up. Their tears stopped at once and they began dancing up and down, shouting, 'Hooray!'

Philip put his finger to his lips to tell them not to make any noise then he shouted, 'Tomorrow. I'll come and get you tomorrow. Nod your heads if you understand.'

They both nodded wildly. He was just about to shout some more when the door opened. The vet had heard the noise and was coming to check. Philip ducked out of sight and ran back to the street.

He walked home slowly, trying to think what he was going to do. He had made a promise to Baby B and Nick, and he would keep it.

But the big problem was – how?

CHAPTER SEVEN

When Philip got home it was quite late and his dad was back from work. During tea he had to listen as his mum told his dad the whole story. When she got to the bit about the vet coming and taking the animals away, Philip found that he couldn't swallow his food. All he could think of was how scared and lonely Baby B and Nick must be, locked up in that cage.

And no matter how hard he racked his brains, he still couldn't work out how he could rescue them. There was no point in trying to explain it all to his parents – they would never believe things about magic and animals who could talk. He would just have to find some other way.

He helped with the washing-up then went upstairs and got ready for bed. The whole time – in the bath, cleaning his teeth, folding his clothes

– he tried to think of a way to persuade the vet to let him have Baby B and Nick. But it was no good.

He got into bed and turned out the light, hoping that he would be able to think better in the dark, but still no ideas came up. Sleep started to drift nearer and nearer. Then, suddenly, he snapped wide awake again.

Mr Edgar's piece of paper! He had forgotten all about it.

He jumped out of bed, switched on the light, and pulled the paper out of his pocket. It was all crushed up and he had to smooth the creases out before he could see it properly.

There was a drawing and, underneath, the words: MESSAGE. STONE POWER RING. He read the words three times, trying to make sense of them, but he couldn't understand what they meant so he looked at the drawing instead.

What could it be? An apple? A watch? At the back of his mind he was sure that it reminded him of something. He turned it upside down, then on its side then back again, but he just couldn't see what it could be.

He looked back at the words. MESSAGE. Could it be a drawing of a microphone? Not really. Or perhaps it was a drawing of a RING. Perhaps you had to put the ring on your finger, like in those fairy stories, and then a wizard or a genie would come. But where was the ring? And did it mean the ring was made out of stone? They were usually made of gold in the stories.

And what did POWER mean? Was it like electricity? Perhaps the drawing was of an electric light bulb. It could be, but how did you get a message through a light bulb?

The questions tumbled round his head but he just couldn't find an answer that seemed to fit. He stared and stared at the paper until his eyes ached and when he finally turned out the light and got into bed again he could still see the drawing in his mind. He was tired, though, and this time nothing came to stop him from sliding into sleep.

It was very, very early when he woke up and as he opened his eyes he felt as if someone had been talking to him in his dreams. He couldn't remember what had been said but it was as if he had been told to wake up because something important was going to happen.

Even though there was still only a faint trace of light in the sky he got out of bed and started dressing. As he pulled his sweater over his head, he caught a glimpse of Mr Edgar's drawing and almost jumped in excitement. Of course, he knew what it was! It was a picture of one of those old stone circles like the one he had seen with his dad when they had gone for a walk on the top of Drevish Moor.

And what the writing meant was that he had to go to a circle of stones like that and he would get a message. Why hadn't he been able to see it last night? It was obvious. And another thing was obvious. He couldn't waste time trying to find a way to make the vet let him have Baby B and Nick. He just had to break in through the window and take them before anyone could stop him.

It all seemed so simple and ten minutes later he quietly opened the back door and slipped out of the house.

He was wearing his warmest clothes and he had his dad's rucksack on his back. He didn't really know why he had picked it up because it was big and clumsy, but a voice in his head had told him that he was going to need it. It was already proving useful because as he had gone through the kitchen he had grabbed as much food as he could and put it inside. In one pocket of his anorak he had all the money from his money box, and in another pocket he had his post office savings book.

As he walked along the side of the house and reached the street, he realized that, without knowing what he had been doing, he had got ready as if he was going to be away for a long time.

He looked up at the closed curtains of the front bedroom. His mum and dad were still asleep there, and Megs was probably still curled up in her usual place downstairs under the table. When would he see them all again?

Philip took one last, long look at his house, then turned and started running down the road.

CHAPTER EIGHT

There had been a heavy frost during the night and Philip's breath steamed as he stood looking at the vet's surgery from the other side of the road. There was no sign of movement on the first two floors and the curtains were shut on the third floor. It was still very early so the vet was probably in bed. Philip crossed the road and ran along the back alley.

He crept up to the back of the vet's house and peered in through the window. It was dark in the room but he could just see the cage and the shapes of Baby B and Nick, curled up asleep.

Somewhere, far off, a dog barked. Apart from the bark and the faint noise of distant traffic, everything was quiet. Breaking the window was going to make a terrible noise. The vet was bound to wake up and it might even wake the neighbours. Supposing someone rang the police? Well, he would just have to be quick.

He unhooked the rucksack from his back and held it by the straps. He would count to three then swing it round and hit the window. One, two, THREE.

CRASH! the whole pane of glass smashed and fell.

Almost before the last piece tinkled to the ground, Philip reached in, slipped the catch, and opened the window. Glass crunched under his feet as he jumped down into the room and at the same time he heard Baby B.

'Oh, Flipip, you breaked the window,' the little beaver said in a shocked voice. 'Will the Mister be angry?'

'I expect so – but if we are very quick, he won't catch us,' Philip said, trying to open the cage.

The catch was stiff and each time he tried to slide it back, his fingers slipped. He tried and failed four times then he heard shouts and the sound of someone running down the stairs. It must be the vet. He tried again, but again his fingers slipped.

'Quick, do it undone!' Baby B shouted.

'He's coming,' squeaked Nick.

Philip dashed to the door and heard footsteps pounding along the corridor. He fumbled with the key and just managed to lock the door in time. The handle turned and then the whole door shook as the vet crashed against it, trying to force it open.

'Open up at once!' yelled the vet and he began

banging on the door, but Philip was already back at the cage, pulling at the catch. This time it slid easily and he swung the wire door open.

'Come on, you two,' he said, and Baby B and Nick scrambled out into his arms. He bent down and undid the flap of his rucksack. The best thing to do would be to put Baby B and Nick inside then lower them gently out of the window before jumping out after them. He had only just tucked them both in, though, when the banging on the door stopped.

Philip listened and heard the vet open another door. There was the sound of footsteps in the back yard – he must be coming round to the window. He would climb in and catch them.

Philip looked round wildly. There was only one way out – through the door. He picked up the rucksack and swung it on to his back.

'Oooh!' Baby B and Nick squealed as they bumped and banged against each other.

'Hold tight!' Philip cried as he ran to the door.

As he turned the key, he heard a shout from behind. He looked and saw the vet starting to climb in through the window. Philip's fingers seemed to go all weak and clumsy and he just couldn't seem to get the door open fast enough. Then, at last, it opened. He pulled the key out, ran into the corridor, slammed the door and locked it.

Now, if they could just find the back door they would be able to run away down the alley before the vet could climb out of the window again. But where was the back door? Philip ran along the corridor and pulled at a door. It opened to show a staircase leading upstairs. That was no good.

Oh, where was the back door? At any minute the vet would get out of the window and they would be trapped.

He ran back down the corridor, past the room, and turned left. Yes, there was the open back door. Quick.

He dashed outside and saw a leg poking out of the window. The vet was climbing out. Philip saw that he was wearing pyjamas and slippers. An idea sprang into his mind. He ran to the window, slid the slipper off the vet's foot and sprinted away as the vet began to yell.

He reached the end of the alley and then looked back. The vet was just coming out of the gate. The alley was very stony and rough and almost at once the vet stopped and lifted his bare foot in agony. The plan had worked.

'You wretched little boy!' the vet screamed as he hopped around, holding on to his foot. 'Come back here. I know who you are, I'll get the police on to you!'

Philip didn't wait to hear more. He threw the slipper over a fence and began to run.

He ran for nearly half a mile before he dared to stop. He was panting hard but he was sure he hadn't been followed.

'Ooh, Flipip,' came Baby B's muffled voice from inside the rucksack, 'it's millions bumpery in here. And Nick is a bit half prickerly when I bumper him.'

'Sorry,' Philip said over his shoulder, 'but I had to run to get away from that vet.'

'Is he coming?'

'No, I think we're safe.'

'Good job – because he is a bit horrible and he didn't give us any tea nor he didn't give us any breakfast.'

'Well,' said Philip, 'if you feel around you'll find some food in there. You can eat that.'

There was silence for quite a long time while Philip walked on, then there was a loud squeak and then some giggles.

'What's going on?' he asked.

There were more giggles and then Baby B finally managed to say, 'It's half very dark in here and Nick was finding some bread and he bit it and it wasn't bread, it was my tail.'

The giggles started again.

'Ssh!' Philip said, trying not to laugh himself. 'We're nearly at the bus station and there will be people around. You must stay very quiet and very still.'

'Where is we going?' Baby B whispered.

'We're going to catch a bus to Drevish Moor. There's a stone circle there and we can send a message to Mr Edgar.'

He tried to make it sound easy so that Baby B and Nick wouldn't worry, but he wasn't nearly as sure as he sounded.

Perhaps he had got Mr Edgar's note all wrong. And perhaps at this very minute the vet was calling the police. If they were caught now he would be in serious trouble and Baby B and Nick would probably be taken away for ever.

CHAPTER NINE

The bus was full and an old lady came to sit next to Philip so he had to put the rucksack on his knee. It was very heavy and after a while he had to move his legs to stop them from going to sleep. As he changed position, the rucksack slipped and he only just managed to catch it.

The sudden movement must have scared Baby B and Nick because they both squeaked and yelped. The old lady tried to pretend that she hadn't heard anything but when the sides of the rucksack began to move as Baby B and Nick moved back into a comfortable position her mouth opened and Philip thought she was going to scream. She didn't, but she began to edge slowly away until she was nearly falling off the seat. Then, as soon as someone got off the bus, she went and sat in their place.

The journey took ages and it was very warm on

the bus and Philip fell asleep for a while. When he woke up the bus was nearly empty and the high, rolling hills outside told him that they couldn't be far from Drevish Moor.

He bent forward, pretending to tie up his shoe-lace, and whispered into the top of the rucksack, 'Not long now.'

'Hooray,' Baby B whispered back. 'It's a bit millions hot in here.'

It wasn't at all hot, ten minutes later, when they got off the bus. The sun was shining but the wind, which was sending the white clouds racing across the sky, was bitterly cold.

'Which is the way to the stone circle, please?' Philip called before the bus drove off.

'Follow that path there,' the driver said, pointing across the road.

The bus chugged away up the hill and Philip crossed the road. The path was steep and stony but he walked quickly for about five minutes then stopped. There was nobody in sight. He took the rucksack off and opened the flap. Baby B and Nick jumped out and stretched themselves.

'Phew that's better. It's too very small in there. Come on, Nick, we can run millions fast.'

They both tore off uphill, Baby B running and skipping with joy and Nick scampering after him. They were so happy to be out in the open air that they shouted and laughed and rolled around in the heather then chased each other up the path.

Halfway up the hill a small stream gurgled and trickled its way across the path and they all stopped to have a drink. The water was icy cold and sweet and it filled them with new strength. Even so, by the time they finally got to the very top of the hill they were all panting hard. Drevish Moor stretched out for miles in front of them. There were no trees or bushes and the wind swept across it, shaking the brown, tufty grass.

'Where is them stones, you said about?' asked Baby B.

'I'm not sure,' said Philip. 'The bus driver said it was somewhere along this path so I suppose we just have to keep going. Come on.'

Although the land was almost flat, the wind blew so fiercely that it was nearly as tiring to walk as it had been to climb the hill. And there was no sign of the stone circle anywhere. Perhaps it was miles away. Philip was just beginning to feel down-hearted when Baby B and Nick started humming a tune. Philip joined in and his spirits rose at once. Somewhere, high above, a bird began singing as if it had heard them and wanted to help the song along.

A few moments later, the birdsong grew louder and when Philip looked up there were five birds hovering in the air off to the right. And now their chirping and tweeting sounded less like a song and more as if they were trying to say something. Almost at once Baby B and Nick bounded off the path and across the wiry grass in the direction of the birds.

'Come on, Flipip, it's this way,' Baby B shouted.

Philip ran after them and, sure enough, a couple of minutes later they reached the top of a slight rise in the ground and saw the stone circle. It lay in a huge hollow and if the birds hadn't shown them where it was they could have easily passed by without seeing it. He raised his head in order to shout 'Thank you' to them, but the sky was empty. A shiver tingled down his spine.

It was like magic.

CHAPTER TEN

The stone circle was enormous – much larger than Philip remembered it from the time he'd seen it with his dad. He counted. There were twenty-four stones in all. Twenty-three of them were as tall as he was but the twenty-fourth was nearly twice his size. He sat down next to Baby B and Nick, pulled Mr Edgar's piece of paper from his pocket, and looked at the drawing.

'Twenty-four. It's exactly the same,' he said when he had finished counting.

Baby B took the paper and pretended to count, though he got a bit mixed up after he got to seven and kept going back to one again. 'See, Nick,' he said at last. 'Twentity-four. It's exactrilly the same.'

'Does it mean we can go back home now?' Nick asked, and he and Baby B turned to look at Philip with big, hopeful eyes.

'Well, perhaps not straight away,' he said gently. 'But I'm sure Mr Edgar meant us to come here, so something is bound to happen.'

He got up and walked down into the circle before they could ask any more awkward questions. He took off his rucksack and started looking at the stones – perhaps the message was written on them.

The stones were very old and some of them were covered with patches of green lichen, but no matter how hard he looked he couldn't see any sign of writing. Baby B and Nick followed him round for a bit but they soon got bored and started playing hide-and-seek among the stones. It took Philip a long time to check all the stones and by the time he got back to where he had started, Baby B and Nick had already tired themselves out and were curled up asleep next to the rucksack.

He pulled the drawing out of his pocket again. This *must* be a STONE POWER RING. It was stone and there were the right number. But what was he supposed to do? It said RING, not CIRCLE. RING. Like a telephone? No, it couldn't be. Perhaps it meant a RINGING sound. He tapped the nearest stone hard but it just made a slapping sound. It couldn't mean that.

Wait a minute, though – what about the X mark on the drawing? It was right in front of the tall stone. He went and peered at the ground in front of the stone, but there was no X marked there, just the same springy grass as everywhere else.

And yet he felt certain that it meant something so he sat down with his back up against the stone.

At once he noticed something. His whole body seemed to be glowing with warmth and he had the oddest feeling, as if he was almost floating. This must be the right place, but now what?

He closed his eyes and spoke quietly, 'Mr Edgar.'

For a moment, the old beaver's face came clearly into his mind and Philip opened his eyes, hoping that he would see Mr Edgar next to him. Nothing. Just the stone circle and Baby B and Nick asleep next to the rucksack.

He closed his eyes and called again, 'Mr Edgar.'

Again he got a picture of Mr Edgar's face, but it faded away as quickly as it had come. He took a deep breath and thought as hard as he could. Mr Edgar. Mr Edgar in Beaver Towers. Mr Edgar, as he remembered him best, sitting in his comfy old chair next to the fire in the library in Beaver Towers.

There was a rushing sound in Philip's ears that grew louder and louder. Then something strange and terrible happened.

Philip's heart stopped beating.

A dreadful cold silence filled his body as the blood stopped moving round it. Then, even before he had time to be scared, there was a sudden jolt in his chest and his heart started pounding again. He felt his blood begin to move but it was as if it was going in the wrong direction. Yes, there was no doubt about it, his blood was going backwards round his body.

At the same time, even though his eyes were still closed, he could see the stone circle begin to spin like a roundabout. Round and round it went, spinning faster and faster until it was just a grey blur and he felt so dizzy he thought he would be sick. Then the grey turned to blue and it was as though he had spun right out of the circle and was flying through the air as fast as the speed of light. The blue turned to a red mist which swirled round him for a moment then suddenly cleared.

He opened his eyes and found himself standing in the library of Beaver Towers.

CHAPTER ELEVEN

Philip blinked. Yes, it was the library of Beaver Towers. Mr Edgar was sitting in front of the fire, just as he had imagined him, and there was a smile on the old beaver's face.

'Well done, young whippersnapper. Well done! I knew you had it in you. I knew it.'

Mr Edgar's voice seemed oddly far away and when Philip spoke even his own voice sounded as if it was coming from a long way off.

'Mr Edgar, what happened? I was in the stone circle with . . .' He stopped and looked around. 'Oh, Mr Edgar, they're not here. Baby B and Nick haven't come.'

'Whoa, whoa! Hold your horses, young lad. No need to get in a tizzy. I'd better do some explaining – always a bit of a shock the first time it happens. Fact is, it might seem as if you're in Beaver Towers with me but you're really sitting in that Power Ring on Drevish Moor.'

Philip could hardly believe his ears. The library seemed so real – he could even feel the heat of the logs crackling away in the fireplace – yet he knew that Mr Edgar was telling the truth.

'But how?' he asked. 'Is it magic?'

'You can call it that if you like,' Mr Edgar said, 'but magic is only a name that people give to things they can't do or they don't understand. You'd think it was magic if you could fly, wouldn't you? But birds do it all the time. What you're doing is something that all human beings could do if they weren't such tomfools. Can you imagine the silly and bad things most people would do with it? Well, luckily, people can only learn how to do it when they can be trusted to use it properly. I always knew you were made of the right stuff – saw it in the brave and sensible way you helped us get rid of that old rotter, Oyin. And most of all, saw it in the way you always thought about others before you thought of yourself.'

'Just a minute, Mr Edgar,' Philip said, trying to take it all in. 'Do you mean that I'm doing the magic?'

' 'Course you are, young 'un. And there are all sorts of marvellous things you'll learn to do if you stick to the right path. But don't you go getting swell-headed because that's the first thing that'll make you lose the power. Remember that this is only your first step: that's why you needed to go to a Power Ring, to give you a bit of a boost.'

'But I don't understand, Mr Edgar. Why did I have to do it? Why didn't you do it?'

A look of sadness passed across Mr Edgar's face. He sighed deeply and brushed his whiskers with his paw and Philip noticed how white the beaver's fur had become since he last saw him.

'That's just the point, young 'un. You're right at the beginning but I'm right at the end. Just an old duffer now – and getting more and more dufferish all the time.'

Mr Edgar's voice was quiet and his eyes lost their sparkle for a moment. Then he slapped his knee and gave a loud chuckle. 'Oh, bless my soul, it was only 'cause I made such a mishmash of things that brought you to Beaver Towers in the first place. Remember?'

Philip nodded and laughed.

'And that didn't turn out so bad, after all,' Mr Edgar went on, his old face beaming and his eyes sparkling again, 'because you were just the tonic we needed. And we need you now – I'll explain why when you get here. But getting you here is where our problems start. I can't help you, you see, because I used up the very last bit of my power sending those rascals Baby B and Nick. I wanted to send the cloud and the dragon kite but I knew I just wouldn't have the power to bring them back, so that was no use. You'll have to call them yourself and I'm afraid your power isn't strong enough to do it yet. Bit of a pickle, eh?'

'So what can I do?' Philip asked, suddenly feeling weak and not at all powerful.

'Our only hope is to get you as near as possible to Beaver Towers. I've been looking at this,' Mr Edgar pointed to a map on his knee, 'and the nearest point of your country to Beaver Towers is a place called . . . Drat, where is it, now? Oh yes – Tarika Head. I want you to get there as quickly as possible. With any luck your power will have got stronger by then and you'll be able to call the kite and the cloud from there.'

'But supposing it isn't? Oh, Mr Edgar, I'm . . .'

Before Philip could finish speaking everything faded away – the library, the fire, Mr Edgar – and he found himself in total darkness.

It was a darkness that was so cold and so still and so black that he felt as if he were lost in space, millions of miles from anywhere, without even the faintest starlight to guide him.

CHAPTER TWELVE

Philip had never felt so alone in his whole life.

Then, with a shiver of horror, he realized that he was not alone. Somewhere, out there, in the terrible night was something darker than darkness. It was coming towards him.

He opened his mouth to scream but no sound came out. Instead, he heard another noise – the slow, awful breathing of some wild beast. It was close now; close enough for him to feel its hot breath blow into his face. He still could not make out its shape, but it was huge – so huge that its blackness had blotted out the blackness of the night sky.

Then, high above him, two eyes flicked open. Two enormous red eyes that glowed as if there were cruel fires burning inside them.

The beast took a deep breath and for a second Philip felt himself sucked towards the hidden mouth, then he was blown backwards by a voice that rumbled like thunder all round him.

'I know you, child. I have been waiting for you. I'm always there – just a step behind you.'

Philip's ears were filled with the terrible roaring sound of the voice. Then, as the last word echoed away, he heard another voice, faint and urgent. It was Mr Edgar.

'Philip! Philip!' the old beaver was calling. 'This is the way. Hold firm, young 'un. Look him in the eyes and laugh at him. You can do it.'

Philip raised his head and forced himself to look at those huge, red, serpent eyes. They stared down at him and he felt as if they could burn him up with their hatred, but he did what Mr Edgar had said. He laughed. It was only a little laugh, weak and nervous, but those big, cruel eyes looked surprised then shocked. It seemed so silly that Philip laughed again, and this time the laugh was real and loud.

The darkness fled away and Philip found himself back in the library, staring at the red glow of two brightly burning logs in the fireplace. A shiver shook him and his teeth began to chatter.

'M-M-Mr Edgar,' he began.

'I know, young 'un, I know,' Mr Edgar said gently. 'Don't worry, the old beast has gone – you sent him packing.'

'Who w-w-was it?'

'The Prince of Darkness. The path is filled with

dangers when you start to use the power. You need to be brave and sensible and good because that old rogue is always lurking around trying to use it for evil things. He tried to scare you off this time by turning up in a horrible shape, but remember that he can come in any shape he wants and he's much more dangerous when he turns up seeming nice and friendly. You must always be on your guard. Bit of a tall order, eh? But I know you can do it.'

The old beaver smiled and took hold of Philip's hand with his paw and gave it a friendly squeeze.

'Ooh my word! Your hand is cold. That's enough power work for one day. You pop back to that stone circle, pick up that scampish grandson of mine and his scampish friend, and then get on your way to Tarika Head. And don't forget – keep a wary, weather-eye open for trouble, and remember what I said about the power being like birds flying. They don't sit around thinking about flying or being proud because they can do it. They just do it when it's useful to do it. Now, off you go. Bye!'

Mr Edgar closed his eyes and Philip opened his own. He was back in the stone circle on Drevish Moor.

Philip's legs were a bit wobbly when he stood up. How long had it all lasted? Baby B and Nick were still asleep so it couldn't have been long, yet it felt as if it had been hours and hours. Anyway Mr Edgar was right about not wasting time thinking about it. Besides, there were some bits he didn't want to remember – like the Prince of Darkness. The very thought of him made Philip go cold and he suddenly felt that he wanted to get away from this lonely moor.

He walked over to Baby B and Nick and said, 'Wake up, sleepyheads.' In a flash their eyes were open and they were bounding round, ready to go. They were full of energy after their sleep and when Philip told them they were going back to the road they went rushing ahead so fast that he had a job to keep up with them.

Then, when they got halfway down the hill, Nick decided that he would try to go even faster. He curled up in a ball and got Baby B to give him a push. The little hedgehog began to spin, faster and faster, until he was racing down the steep hill at breakneck speed. Philip knew that the grass and the heather were soft but he held his breath in case Nick bumped against one of the rocks sticking up. He needn't have worried, though. At the bottom, Nick rolled to a stop, uncurled himself, and ran around calling to Baby B to do it.

Baby B tried to curl himself up into a ball but his big beaver tail kept getting in the way so he lay on his side and started to roll down like that. His fat tummy helped and he had soon whirled and bounced his way down to where Nick was waiting. At once they began chasing each other and their laughs and shouts drifted up the hill to

Philip. They were so lively and full of fun and he was really glad that they would be there to share the dangers of the journey with him. After all, if the Prince of Darkness was just a step behind all the time . . .

Just as that thought came into his mind, the wind howled, bitingly cold, down from the moor. He turned quickly and, although all he could see was the tall grass and the heather shaking in the wind, he had the horrible feeling that there were eyes peering at him from every hiding place.

He started to run and he didn't stop until he was safe with his friends at the bottom of the hill.

CHAPTER THIRTEEN

They waited at the bus stop, with Philip sitting next to the rucksack and Baby B and Nick inside it so that they could duck down and hide whenever a car came by. In fact, hardly any cars went past and Philip began to be a bit worried because he didn't like the idea of being stuck in such a lonely place when it got dark. Already the sun was going down behind the hills.

'I wonder when the brush will come,' Baby B said.

Philip laughed. 'It's not a brush, it's a bus.'

Baby B and Nick practised saying the word 'bus' for a while, then the little beaver asked, 'Where is we going to on the *bus*, Flipip?'

'Wherever it goes to. And then we've got to go to a place called Tarika Head. I'm not even sure where it is, except that it's near the sea so it must be a long way away.'

'The sea, hooray,' shouted Baby B. 'I can do my swimming.'

'I don't want to do my swimming,' Nick said. 'I like rolling best.'

A big lorry came chug-chugging its way up the hill towards them so the two animals slid down into the rucksack. Philip wondered if he dared to put his thumb out and try to get a lift, but he remembered how his mum and dad said it was very dangerous to go off with a stranger so he sat still and watched the lorry roar past. Oh, if only the bus would come. The sun had gone and the dark was beginning to creep across the sky.

'Flipip,' Baby B asked as he and Nick stood up again, 'why is we going to that Treacle Head place what you said?'

'Mr Edgar told me we had to.'

'Grandpa Edgar!' Baby B squeaked. 'Hooray! Is he come to see us?'

'Not exactly,' Philip said, not quite sure how to explain what had happened. 'He's still at Beaver Towers but I had a sort of talk with him. It was all a bit strange, really.'

'I bet you did think-talking, didn't you?' Baby B said and then turned to Nick. 'I bet he did think-talking, Nick, don't you?'

'Do you know about it then?' Philip asked, surprised.

''Course we do, don't we, Nick? It's where you thinking of someone and then you do talking to them even if they is millions away. Grandpa Edgar told us about it and he says if we be good we can to do it when we be a bit older, only about five or six. And me and Nick try to do it, don't we?' Nick nodded and Baby B went on, getting excited. 'Nick goes in another room when I'm in another room what's not the same room as his room and then we think and sometimes we can do it, can't we?'

There was a long pause then Nick shook his head and whispered, 'Oh, Baby B, you telled a fibber. We can't.'

Baby B glanced at Philip and then ducked down into the rucksack to hide. A moment later he popped up again with his paws over his eyes. 'Well, we can a bit nearly,' he mumbled, 'so it's not a big, big fibber, is it?' He peeked out from behind his paws to see if Philip was angry. Even though Philip smiled, to show that he wasn't, Baby B kept his paws over his eyes.

'I know, let's play a game,' Philip said to try and change the subject.

'Yes! Let's do rolling,' Nick shouted.

'No, I think we'd better stay here in case the bus comes,' Philip said, then tried to think of games they could do without moving. It was hard, though – they couldn't play 'Noughts and Crosses' because they didn't have pencils and paper, and Baby B and Nick couldn't do 'I Spy With My Little Eye' because they didn't know the letters of

the alphabet properly for the 'Something Beginning With' bit.

'We could do "Stoats and Weasels",' Nick said.

'What's that?' Philip asked.

'It's easy,' Baby B said, forgetting about his fibber at last and jumping up and down with excitement. 'Somebody says a thing and then somebody
else says a thing like it. Like if Nick says "Rabbit",
I can say "Hare" and that's right, but if Nick says
"Flea" I can't say "Owl" because that's not right.
It's easy.'

Philip had to agree that it sounded easy, even
if it didn't sound very interesting.

'All right, then, who's going to start?' he asked.

'Me, me,' cried Baby B. 'I'm going to do a good
one. Um . . . I know. Parrot.'

'Stoats and weasels,' Nick said in a funny voice.

'That's not right, Nick,' Baby B began. 'Parrots
isn't like . . .'

'No, really – stoats and weasels, look!' Nick
squeaked then dived to the bottom of the rucksack.

Baby B and Philip looked. It was hard to see
much in the gloom but what Philip could make
out was scaring enough. The ground on the side
of the hill seemed to be moving. Baby B gasped
and dropped down into the rucksack alongside
Nick. Then Philip saw that it wasn't the ground
moving – it was hundreds of long, thin animals
snaking and weaving their way down the hillside.

Nick was right, they were stoats and weasels.

Philip grabbed the rucksack and swung it up on to his back. As he did so, the leader, a large stoat, reached the road and stopped. The others came to a halt behind. At once the weasels stood up on their hind legs, but the stoats stayed on all fours with their black-tipped tails swishing angrily.

Philip stepped forward and clapped his hands loudly. 'Shoo! Shoo! Shoo!' he shouted.

Some of the animals turned tail and ran off a little way but most of them opened their mouths and hissed and snarled at him so that he could see their needle-sharp teeth. He knew at once that they had been sent by the Prince of Darkness.

Suddenly the leader darted across the road and snapped at Philip's leg. Philip felt the stoat's teeth just miss his skin but when he looked down the savage creature was still hanging on to his jeans. He kicked out wildly and the stoat lost his grip and sailed right across the road to land in a heap in the middle of the others. For a moment they turned to look at their leader and Philip began to run.

He ran madly, faster than he had ever run before, away down the road. But even as he ran, he knew there was nowhere to run to. In a matter of seconds they would catch up with him and knock him to the ground. He could already hear their scampering feet behind him and he could feel his legs beginning to tire.

Then, just as he had given up hope, lights

flashed in his eyes. The bus was coming. It had swept round the corner at the bottom of the hill and was starting to climb up to him. If he could just keep going . . .

He clenched his fists and made his legs pound away faster than ever but the bus had slowed down now that it had got to the steep bit of the hill and those horrible animals were right at his heels. He could feel their sharp teeth snapping at the back of his shoes.

Suddenly there was a loud blast from the horn as the driver saw him. The scampering feet stopped and when Philip glanced over his shoulder he saw the stoats and weasels darting off into the darkness on either side of the road. There was an even louder blast from the horn and he heard the squeal of tyres as the bus jerked to a halt a few feet away from him.

'You silly little boy, you'll get yourself killed running down the middle of the road like that,' the driver said as Philip climbed on to the bus.

'Sorry,' Philip panted. 'I thought you wouldn't stop.'

'Yeah, nearly stopped over your dead body,' the driver said.

'I know,' Philip said, but he wasn't thinking of being run over by the wheels of the bus, he was thinking of hundreds of long, snaky bodies with their slashing teeth.

'Well,' asked the driver, 'where do you want to go?'

'To Hoo, please,' Philip replied, glad that he had seen the name on the front of the bus before he had got on.

He paid his money, went to the rear of the empty bus, took off his rucksack and sat down on the back seat. The bus began to grind its way to the top of the hill. Philip looked out of the window and saw the lights from the bus reflecting in hundreds of eyes that peered from the darkness at the side of the moor. Then the bus gathered speed and the eyes were left behind.

Philip leaned down to the rucksack next to him on the seat and whispered. 'We're safe.'

And for a moment, at least, they were.

CHAPTER FOURTEEN

It was very dark and very cold by the time they reached the small town of Hoo. Philip stood in the old market square as the bus drove away and looked round him. All the shops were closed and the streets were empty. The only place that he had seen open was a petrol station that they had passed on their way into town and he set off in that direction.

There was some bumping and wriggling in the rucksack and then Baby B whispered, 'Flipip, where is we going?'

'I'm going to a petrol station to buy a map to see how to get to Tarika Head. And you must be very quiet because we're nearly there.'

Philip walked past the petrol pumps towards the brightly-lit shop. This was going to be danger-ous. For all he knew, the police might have put his picture on television or in the newspapers.

After all, he had run away from home and the vet had probably told them about breaking the window and stealing Baby B and Nick.

The garage man hardly looked up from his newspaper as Philip went in. The maps were in a rack next to the cans of oil and he picked one up and walked over to pay for it. It cost much more than he had expected but he quickly took some money out of his pocket, gave it to the man, and turned towards the door.

'Hey!' the man called.

Philip jumped in fright. Was his picture in the newspaper?

'Don't go without your change,' the man said.

Philip's hand shook as he held it out but the man just dropped the coins into it and went back to reading his paper. Philip forced himself to walk calmly to the door and away into the night.

Well, that was one problem solved – he had a map – but the next problem wasn't going to be so easy. Where were they going to spend the night? It was very, very cold and the road was shiny with frost. They would freeze to death if they had to stay outdoors all night. Even now he could feel the cold air biting his face. All the houses they were passing looked so warm and cosy with the people sitting round the firesides.

He walked fast and soon arrived back at the square. Now where? There were three roads leading off the square and he did 'Dip, Dip, Dip, My

Little Ship' to see which one to take. While he was doing it he hoped that he wouldn't choose the dark, narrow lane on the left but at the end of the rhyme he found his finger pointing to it. Oh, never mind, this was the one that had been chosen and it might bring him luck.

It didn't.

He turned the corner and walked straight into a policeman.

'Ouf!' said the policeman, as Philip's head butted his tummy.

'Ouch!' said the policeman as Philip's feet trod on his toes.

Before the policeman had time to recover Philip shouted 'Sorry!' then dodged to the left and tore off down the lane. A moment later he heard the stamp and click of boots as the policeman started to run after him.

Philip's brain was racing as fast as his feet. What could he do? At any minute the policeman would catch up with him and take him to the police station. They would ask questions and look in the rucksack and he would probably be sent home. Baby B and Nick would be taken back to the vet and they would never get to Tarika Head.

The heavy rucksack bounced around on his back and Philip could feel Baby B and Nick being shaken and tumbled around inside.

'Oh! Ooh! Ouch!' they were calling.

'Come back! Stop!' the policeman was shouting

and the sound of his boots was echoing down the lane.

It was hardly any wonder that dogs began to bark and, as he ran, Philip could see people come to their windows to find out what all the row was about. Then, on top of all this noise, a clock began to strike loudly.

Philip glanced to the side and saw a church. He pushed open the gate and dashed into the church-yard. He ran up the path, cut across some grass, and ducked down behind a dark shape. It was only when he looked and saw all the other dark shapes in rows around him that he realized that they must be gravestones. He was kneeling on a grave.

It gave him a cold, shivery shock, but before he could move, the church clock stopped striking and he heard the crunch of boots on the path near him. It was the policeman.

Philip held his breath.

'All right,' said the policeman, 'come out. I know you're there somewhere.'

The light from a torch flashed across the grave-stones and when it moved away Philip almost wished it would come back because it was so creepy and dark without it.

The policeman's footsteps moved on towards the church then there was a thud and the tinkle of glass.

'Oh, blast!' the policeman said and Philip real-ized that he had dropped the torch. Philip, heard him pick it up and click the switch. The clicking sound came about six times and then the policeman said, 'Blast!' again. The torch must be broken.

Perhaps if he stayed very still, the policeman wouldn't find him in the dark.

There was a long silence, then the policeman spoke again, 'Now listen to me. You'd better come out at once. I'll wait here all night if I have to.' His voice wobbled a bit and Philip almost had to laugh because he could tell that although the policeman was trying to sound brave he didn't really like the idea of being in a dark graveyard without a torch.

At once an idea began to form in Philip's mind. Baby B and Nick were experts at moving around without making any noise. If they could just creep up behind the policeman, they might be able to scare him enough to send him away.

He quietly slid the rucksack off his back, lifted the flap, and whispered his plan. Baby B started to giggle with excitement at the plan and Philip had to put his hand over the little beaver's mouth.

'Ready?' he whispered when Baby B had finally stopped giggling. The two animals nodded their heads and padded off into the night, moving so quietly that Philip couldn't even hear the grass rustle.

He counted to a hundred, then added another twenty just in case. They must be ready by now. He stood up. The policeman had his back to him so he took a deep breath and shouted, 'Help!'

The policeman spun round so fast that he almost fell over.

'Help!' Philip shouted again.

'What's the matter?' the policeman asked.

Baby B and Nick timed it perfectly. Philip saw something small and dark run out from behind a grave and it almost made him jump until he saw that it was Nick.

The little hedgehog's voice was very high and squeaky as he rushed towards the policeman shouting, 'Eeeeeeeeeeeeeeeh!'

The poor man took one look at this strange shape racing towards him and leapt straight into the air.

For one awful moment Philip thought that the policeman would land right on top of Nick but by the time the man's boots crunched down on the gravel the little hedgehog had disappeared into the dark.

'Wh-wh-what was that?' the policeman asked, and his voice was nearly as squeaky as Nick's.

Almost before he had finished speaking he let out a cry as Baby B jumped on to the top of a grave next to him.

'Whooooooooooooooo!' moaned Baby B, waving his arms and slapping his tail loudly on the ground. 'Whoooooooo! Whoooooooooooooooo! Whoooooooooooooooo!'

At that moment Nick came scuttling back across

the path going, 'Eeeeeeeeeeeeeeeeeeeeeeeeeeh!'

They both looked and sounded very scary and it was all too much for the policeman. He threw his hands in the air and dashed away down the path, he skidded out of the gate and raced off up the lane so fast that within seconds the clomp and clatter of his boots had faded away into the distance.

Even though the policeman had gone, there was no time to waste. At any minute he might be back, and he might bring other policemen with him. Philip darted to the path, put Baby B and Nick into the rucksack, then swung it on to his back and hurried to the gate. He peered up the lane. It was empty. He checked once more then began to run, run like the wind.

Down the lane. Turn left. Down a street. Turn right. Down another street. Left again. On and on until he came to the edge of the town.

Ahead lay the dark countryside and Philip finally stopped. He leaned against a fence and waited until his racing heart slowed down and his lungs stopped gasping for air. Even then his body was so tired that all he wanted to do was fall to the ground and rest but he forced himself to stand up straight. There was a popping noise in his ear and then he heard the music.

It was faint but beautiful; so beautiful that Philip found himself following it without really knowing what he was doing. It led him away from the town into the dark countryside, then up along a small track towards some trees. In the middle of the trees stood a small wooden barn. The door of the barn was open and out of it came the soft beautiful music and a warm glowing light.

As Philip reached the door, the music faded and stopped. He peeped into the barn and saw someone sitting at a bench with their back towards him.

'Don't just stand there in the cold. Come in,' said the person.

It was a funny kind of voice – deep and a bit growly – but it didn't sound like a man's voice. And how had the person known he was there without turning round to see?

Philip knew it could be a trap. Perhaps a trap set by the Prince of Darkness. But he whispered, 'Don't make any noise,' to Baby B and Nick, then he went in.

CHAPTER FIFTEEN

From the outside the barn had looked like a place for keeping animals or farm machines, but inside it wasn't like that at all. The first half of it, up to the bench, was like a carpenter's workshop. There was a cement floor covered with sawdust and wood chippings, and there were racks of tools along the walls. Piles of large logs were stacked just inside the door, and around the benches stood lots of wooden carvings of people and animals. They were smooth and gleaming with polish and Philip felt that it would be nice to run his hands over them.

Beyond the bench, it was completely different. Although the walls were painted white it was the most colourful room he had ever seen. There were pictures and brightly coloured rugs on the wall. The floor was made of light blue tiles and he could hardly see the roof because of all the bunches of dried flowers that were hanging down. A big metal stove stood at the far end of the room and it was glowing with heat. The warm air was filled with the delicious scent of wood and polish and herbs and flowers.

The person at the bench swung round and Philip saw that it was a woman. She was dressed in jeans and a big, baggy sweater and her smiling face was reddy-brown. She had dark, curly hair that had streaks of grey in it; she was wearing glasses, and two huge wooden earrings hung from her ears.

'Come right in,' she said, 'and make yourself at home. I'll be finished in a couple of ticks. You can take your weight off your legs over there.'

She pointed to an area on the other side of the bench and, as Philip made his way there, she picked up a guitar and began playing. The music was the same calm, beautiful sound that he had heard outside.

He took off his rucksack and sat down on one of the enormous cushions that were scattered all over the floor. The sides of the rucksack bulged as Baby B and Nick moved around to get comfortable, so he pulled it so that it would be hidden behind his legs. When he got it into place he glanced up and saw the woman looking at him. She smiled and went on playing the guitar. Her fingers only just seemed to brush the strings lightly but the barn was filled with the lovely sound.

When she finally stopped, Philip wanted to ask

her to go on but she held up the guitar and said, 'That'll do. Took me a week, but it's finished. What do you think of it?'

'It's lovely,' he said. 'Did you make it?'

'Indeed I did,' she said, putting the guitar down on the bench and getting up and walking towards him. 'Always wanted to have a bash at doing one. Now, then, how about something to eat? Are you hungry?'

Philip was just about to say yes, when his empty tummy rumbled very loudly.

The woman laughed. 'Your belly speaks louder than your mouth – and it never lies. And what about your pet? And don't make your mouth lie now, because I know you've got something in that rucksack. What is it? A cat? A Dog?'

Philip's mouth fell open and he didn't know what to say. How did she know so much?

'Nothing to it,' the woman said, as if he had asked the question out loud. 'Everybody would know a lot more about things if only they kept their eyes and ears open and asked themselves more questions. For instance, I only need to take one look at the way you're dressed and see your rucksack and that map sticking out of your pocket to know that you don't intend to go home tonight. Then I only have to notice the rucksack move to know that there is something alive in there. And when I see you handle it gently I know that you must care about whatever is inside it. And I look at the way you wiped your shoes when you came in and the way you sat down carefully and I know that you must be sensible and considerate. Now, caring and sensible and considerate people don't do things to hurt people, so I know that there must be a very good reason why you aren't going home. Am I right?'

Philip nodded.

'There you are, then. Just by looking I found out a lot about you. And the funny thing is that the more closely you look at people and work things out about them, the easier it is to tell what they are thinking. Now, if you do the same thing about me, you might know what I'm thinking. Have a go.'

Philip looked at her and thought of all the things she had said and done since he had come in and then he closed his eyes and tried to put it all together to see what she was thinking. He had only just closed his eyes, when her voice came loud and clear, but he knew that she wasn't speaking – the words were inside her head.

'You're thinking that I can stay here for the night if I want to,' Philip said, opening his eyes.

'Exactly. Well? Do you want to?'

'Yes, please,' Philip said.

'Good. By the way, my name is Bridget, but everyone calls me Birdie. What's yours?'

'Philip.'

'That's a good name – it means "Someone who

loves horses". You probably love other animals too. Right then, Philip, let's have something to eat.'

CHAPTER SIXTEEN

Birdie made the best salad Philip had ever tasted. There were nuts and apples and raisins and carrots and celery and all sorts of other things in a tasty dressing, and two lumps of crumbly cheese with crisp, warm bread.

'I make the bread myself and the cheese comes from the farm next door,' Birdie said when Philip told her how much he liked it.

The rest of the time they ate in silence. It was a nice kind of silence, though, and it gave Philip a chance to think. He had only just met Birdie but already he felt that she was wise and gentle and he knew that he could trust her. And what she had said about being able to know what people were thinking – that was almost like the think-talking he had done with Mr Edgar. Perhaps she knew how to do it, too. Mr Edgar had said that most human beings couldn't do it because they would use it for bad or silly things, but Philip was sure that Birdie wouldn't use it like that.

'Well, that's our hunger taken care of,' Birdie said, as she put her empty plate on the floor next to Philip's and lit a small cigar. 'But what about that pet of yours? He must still be hungry.'

Philip looked down at the rucksack. This was going to be difficult. He was sure that he could trust Birdie but even she would probably find it hard to believe that animals could talk. The best thing to do was to try to warn Baby B and Nick so that they would keep quiet.

'There are two of them,' he said. 'A beaver and a hedgehog.'

'Oh?' Birdie said. 'How exciting. They're very unusual pets to keep.'

'Well, they're more than pets, really. They're ever so clever. I'm sure they understand things I say to them. Sometimes I even think they would like to talk to me. It's a pity animals can't talk, isn't it?' Philip said, making the 'can't talk' bit as loud as possible.

'Animals have their own special way of telling us things,' Birdie said, getting up. 'I'll go and get some nuts and apples and carrots – I expect they'll like them.'

As she went off to the other side of the room, Philip undid the rucksack and lifted Baby B and Nick out. He didn't dare say anything, in case Birdie heard, so he just put his finger to his lips to tell them not to say anything. Baby B nodded and sat down on the floor next to Nick. They looked round the room and then looked at each other. Philip prayed that they wouldn't start giggling.

'Oh, there they are,' Birdie said, coming back with a bowl of salad. 'Aren't they lovely. And doesn't the beaver look smart in those splendid dungarees.'

She put the bowl of salad in front of Baby B and Nick and then sat down on a cushion opposite Philip. Baby B picked up an apple and began to eat it and Nick pushed his snout into the bowl and started eating nuts.

Birdie laughed and said, 'Well, you certainly seem to like the salad. I bet you were both hungry, weren't you?'

Baby B looked up and nodded.

Birdie clapped her hands in surprise. 'You're right, Philip. They do seem to understand. You do understand, don't you?' she said to Baby B and Nick.

Baby B finished his mouthful quickly and said, 'We is very clever at understanding but we can't do talking, can we Nick, because we is animals.'

'Yes,' Nick mumbled, still crunching a nut. 'We can't do talking because we is animals.'

Philip coughed loudly and glanced across at Birdie, hoping that by some piece of luck she hadn't heard. But it was obvious that she had. She was staring at Baby B and Nick, shaking her head in wonder. 'That's amazing,' she said, at last. 'Absolutely amazing. They talked. I heard a beaver and a hedgehog talk!'

There was a silence. Baby B and Nick had gone on eating happily but now they stopped and looked, first at Birdie, then at Philip, then at each other.

'Oh, Baby B,' Nick said as if they had been caught doing something naughty.

Baby B looked up to Philip and said in a loud whisper, 'We told her we can't do talking but she doesn't believe us.'

It was so funny that Philip couldn't help it, he just sat back and roared with laughter. Birdie clapped her hands and joined in. It didn't take long for Baby B and Nick to see the joke and soon all four of them were roaring with laughter.

'Oh dear me,' Birdie said at last, wiping tears from her eyes, 'I haven't laughed like that for ages. And now that your secret is out, Philip, I would very much like to be properly introduced to your amazing friends. And then, if you think you can trust me, I'd like to know some more about what you are doing.'

Philip introduced Baby B and Nick and they both shyly stepped forward and gave her a paw to shake. Birdie said that she would be honoured if they would let her make some drawings of them while they finished eating. They said they wouldn't mind at all so, while they ate, Birdie got some pencils and paper and began to draw. And while she drew, Philip started to tell her about all his adventures. He began at the very beginning when he had first been carried away to Beaver Towers on the dragon kite and he went through everything right up to the moment that he had followed the music to Birdie's farm.

It was a long, long story and by the time he finished Baby B and Nick had finished eating and had curled up on a cushion and gone to sleep. Birdie was wide awake, though. At first she had listened and drawn at the same time but, by and by, she put the paper down and put her arms around her legs and listened to him with her chin resting on her knees.

There was a long silence when Philip came to the end of the story.

'Don't you believe me?' he asked.

'Certainly, I believe you,' she said. 'I know that every word you've told is the truth. Most people wouldn't believe you, of course, but that's because most people go through their lives as if they were asleep. It's like being able to read thoughts – most people think that it's some kind of magic instead of seeing that everybody could do it if only they woke up. No, there are lots and lots of things that human beings don't understand yet. But what worries me, young man, is you. Tarika Head is a long way away and now that the Prince of Darkness has become interested in you, it's going to be a journey filled with danger.'

Philip shivered and suddenly felt very cold and achy and tired. Birdie saw the shiver and got up at once.

'Anyway, you must be exhausted. It's very late and time we were all asleep like Baby B and Nick. We can sort out what to do tomorrow when the bright light of tomorrow comes. Now then, let's get these two covered up first.'

She got some blankets and laid them gently on Baby B and Nick then she pushed some cushions together and made a big comfortable bed for Philip. She gave him a sleeping bag and then busied herself, closing the barn door and clearing up. Philip slipped off his clothes and got into the pyjamas Birdie had lent him. They were much too big but he didn't care. All he wanted to do was to lie down and sleep. As he got into the sleeping bag another shiver shook him.

Birdie came across and tucked him up then put her hand on his face.

'Hmm,' she said, 'you're a bit hot, lad. I hope you're not sickening for something. Anyway, close your eyes and get some sleep. You're quite safe here – old Birdie will look after you.'

Philip closed his eyes and was asleep at once.

CHAPTER SEVENTEEN

Philip was ill.

His whole body ached and he moved around in the bed trying to get comfortable but he couldn't. Even his skin ached. He was hot. His face burned with a dry heat that made his head throb, but his body was wet with sweat. He pulled and pulled at the zip of the sleeping bag with weak achy fingers. Finally he opened it and threw it off him. For a few moments he felt cool and free, then he grew cold and shivery and his teeth rattled so he pulled the bag back on top of him and the burning heat began again. He groaned and moaned, and each groan and moan helped for a few seconds.

A nurse came towards him. She seemed to be floating, then he realized that she was wearing roller skates. Why was she wearing roller skates? She skated round and round his bed until he felt dizzy then she stopped and pulled some pills from her pocket. They were a horrible colour and they were much too big to swallow. Then, as she held them out, he saw that they had a skull and crossbones on them. They were poison. He lifted his hand to knock them away and the nurse changed to the Prince of Darkness. He was dressed like a nurse but his head was just a skull with grinning teeth.

A light flicked on and hurt his eyes so he closed them and moaned again. Someone's cool hand touched his face, and a voice – was it his mum's or Birdie's? – talked to him but he couldn't really hear anything except, 'Drink it. Come on, drink up.' A glass was pressed against his lips and he gulped and gulped. Water. Cool water. The light went out and he slept.

Then he woke and his bed was soaking wet with sweat and he wanted to cry but he couldn't. All he could do was moan. He felt the sleeping bag being lifted off him and soft sheets were put on top of him and blankets were tucked round him. And he slept.

He woke – it was a grey, early morning light and he felt weak – oh, so weak and achy. He closed his eyes and his head pounded and his ears hissed and there were tiny men running round on his bed and they were banging drums and he wanted them to go away. But perhaps the drums were a sort of think-talking sent by Mr Edgar and he couldn't understand. And the drums beat on. And he slipped into sleep.

Someone was stroking his hand. He opened his eyes. The barn door was open and he could hear noises. He looked to see who was touching his hand. It was Baby B.

'Oh, Flipip, you is ill,' Baby B said.

'I know,' Philip said. Then he let Baby B's gentle stroking send him back to sleep.

The aching got worse and worse and the burning got hotter and hotter and Philip tossed and turned and moaned and groaned. The sweat soaked his pyjamas and his sheets.

Hands lifted him off the bed and took his pyjamas off and he felt a warm flannel washing all the heat and the sweat away. Cool, dry pyjamas were put on him and then a voice said, 'Lie down.' He sat on the floor – he hadn't got the strength to open his eyes and find the bed.

Then another voice – it was definitely Baby B's, said, 'Oh Flipip, stand up. You is in the floor.'

'*On* the floor,' he whispered and then laughed weakly as hands lifted him and laid him down on a soft, cool bed. Sheets were placed over him and, as he drifted off to sleep, he knew the fever had gone.

CHAPTER EIGHTEEN

Philip could feel himself coming back from a long way away. There was a soft tap-tapping noise and two voices were humming a tune. The hum came to an end and the two voices started singing. It was Baby B and Nick, and Philip couldn't help smiling as he listened to their song:

Run to Beaver Towers, run to Beaver Towers,
Through the wind and through the showers
It might take us hours and hours
To get back to Beaver Towers.

'That really is a lovely song,' Birdie said.
'We is going to make up some more,' Baby B said, 'because we finded some new words to go with "Towers", didn't we, Nick?'
'Yes, but we must sing it quiet because Flipip is all asleep,' Nick whispered loudly.

Philip opened his eyes and slowly turned his head. 'No, I'm not,' he said, and he found that his throat was very dry and his voice sounded croaky.

'Flipip!' Baby B shouted and rushed to the side of the bed. 'Is you a bit all better?'

'Much. Much better,' Philip said, trying to sit up but finding that he was still too weak.

'Well, well,' Birdie said, coming over to him. 'Now don't rush things. You've been very ill – three whole days you've been lying there. You're going to feel a bit droopy and feeble for a while – but I've got just the thing to get you on your feet again.'

She went away and came back with a tall glass full of a purple drink.

'It's full of all sorts of good things – herbs and honey and juices from berries – so drink it all up.'

Philip had never tasted anything like it. It was bitter and sweet at the same time and as soon as he swallowed it he could feel it warming his insides and giving him strength.

Birdie smiled and said, 'That's good. In about an hour's time you'll be ready for some food. I've got some delicious soup bubbling away over there. But meanwhile I've got a bit of work to finish on my carving of Baby B and Nick. Come on, you two – get back in position.'

Birdie picked up a hammer and chisel and began tapping softly at the wood. Philip lay and listened to the tap-tapping and soon Baby B and Nick began humming and singing their song again. Baby B had added the new words.

Run to Beaver Towers, run to Beaver Towers,
Past the trees and past the flowers.
We is using all our powers
To get us back to Beaver Towers.

They sang it over and over and even Birdie joined in as she tapped at the wood. Philip listened and thought. Yes, they had to use all their powers to get back to Beaver Towers. They had lost three whole days while he had been ill – Mr Edgar must be wondering what had happened to them.

He reached over and picked up the map which was lying on top of his clothes next to the bed. He opened it up and began looking for Tarika Head. He ran his finger along the line on the map where the blue sea met the green land and at last he found it. Now, where was Hoo? He looked for ages before he saw it. Gosh, it was a long way – and in between the two places there was an area of purple and white marked on the map that showed that they would have to cross very high mountains. How were they going to do it?

Philip was still trying to work out the way they would have to go when the tapping stopped and Birdie came across to him.

'Looking at the map, eh? I've had a look, too. It's quite some journey, isn't it?'

Philip nodded.

'Never mind, you'll do it, lad. And I've got a plan to help you on your way. The farmer who lives over the fields often goes to the mountains in his lorry to deliver milk. He's an old friend of mine and I'm sure he'll give you a lift. I'll just pour the soup then I'll pop over and ask him.'

Birdie brought a huge bowl of steaming soup for Philip and two smaller bowls for Baby B and Nick.

'Right, you three – this will build you up and fill you full of energy. Eat it all up. I'll be back in a few ticks.'

The soup was absolutely delicious and they all kept saying, 'Mmm, it's lovely,' as they ate.

'Mmm, that's lovely,' Baby B said once more as he licked up the last drop from his bowl. Then he and Nick ran over to the work bench and came back carrying the carving that Birdie had been doing. They held it up for Philip to see.

'It's beautiful,' Philip said. And it was. It looked just like them and Birdie had done it so well that the wooden Nick had prickles that stood up, just like they did on the real Nick.

'Ah, looking at my little woodwork,' Birdie said, as she came in through the barn door. 'What do you think of it?'

'It's fantastic,' Philip said.

'Oh, it's not bad. It will be a nice thing to remind me of these two scamps when you've gone. I wish you could stay longer but Jim tells me he's off to the mountains tomorrow so I suppose you'll have to go with him because he won't be going again for another week. Do you think you'll be up to it, Philip?'

Philip nodded and smiled.

'That's the spirit, lad. There's not much that will hold you back.'

'But, Birdie,' Baby B said, 'you haven't got a crarving of Flipip, like the crarving of us.'

Birdie smiled. 'Oh, I won't need one of him,' she said, looking at Philip and winking. 'All I'll have to do is think of him and I'll see him clearly enough. Right, Philip?'

'Yes,' he said softly because he felt sad at the idea of going.

'Good. Now, off to sleep all of you. You'll have to be up early tomorrow and you've got a big day ahead of you.'

CHAPTER NINETEEN

It was still dark when Birdie woke them up. They got dressed and then tucked into a huge breakfast while Birdie made some sandwiches and packed them into the rucksack.

'I hope I've left enough room for Baby B and Nick,' she laughed when she finished. She sat down and drank a big mug of tea while they ate the rest of their breakfast. 'Right,' she said, 'time to get moving and time to say goodbye.'

Baby B's eyes began to fill with tears as she bent down and gave him a kiss.

'Bye, Birdie,' he sniffed. 'Thank you for having us.'

'My pleasure, you little rascal, my pleasure.'

'Thank you for having us,' Nick said, and then rolled up into a ball so that nobody could see that he was crying too.

'Oh, dear,' said Birdie, taking off her glasses

and blowing her nose, 'it's always so sad saying goodbye.'

Just then there was the noise of the lorry pulling up outside so Philip popped Baby B and Nick into the rucksack.

'That'll be Jim,' Birdie said. 'Now Philip, dear, are you feeling up to it?'

'Yes, honestly, Birdie. I'm much better.'

'Fighting fit – that's the idea. Now you look after yourself and those two young scamps. Jim will take you right to the other side of the mountains so you'll be well on your way to Tarika Head. Don't be surprised if he doesn't do much talking, though – he's a man of few words, is Jim.'

She gave Philip a quick hug and he thanked her for all she had done, then they went out of the barn.

The big milk lorry stood chugging just outside the door and Philip climbed up into the cab and put the rucksack down on the floor next to his feet.

'Look after this lad, Jim. He's a good friend of mine,' Birdie shouted as she slammed the door.

'Will do,' the farmer replied. And then they were off.

Philip leaned out of the window and waved as the lorry bounced down the bumpy track. Birdie waved back and then turned and walked into the barn.

The lorry roared along the empty roads with its yellow headlamps shining into the dark blue early morning light. Birdie had been right, Jim was a man of very few words indeed. In fact, apart from the occasional cry of 'Whoops' whenever the lorry hit a bump and all the milk churns clattered and clanked, he didn't say a word.

At last the sky grew lighter and Philip looked out at the misty fields rushing past. The sun came up, turning the mist red and finally melting it away to show the countryside fresh and clean and sparkling. The lorry raced on, rolling up hill and down dale. Then, suddenly, they got to the top of one hill and there, ahead of them, were the mountains. Their glistening snowy peaks reached up towards the clear blue sky.

Philip got out his map and traced the red line that showed where the road went. If Jim took them all the way to the other side of the mountains they would be very near Tarika Head. Perhaps, if they were lucky, they would make it before this evening. Then, if everything went right, he could call the cloud and the dragon kite and by tomorrow they would be safe in Beaver Towers.

He was so excited that he couldn't help smiling and he turned to Jim and said, 'It's a lovely day, isn't it?'

The farmer grunted and said, 'Hmm, is it? Take a look at that.'

Philip couldn't understand how anyone could be so grumpy on such a beautiful day but when he looked out of the windscreen he knew what Jim meant. A moment ago the sky had been clear and blue but now, as if out of nowhere, huge black clouds were racing up from behind the mountains. It had happened so quickly that Philip blinked in surprise and then a strange cold feeling ran down his back. A zigzag of lightning forked out of the clouds.

'It's a storm,' Jim said, and shifted in his seat as if he wanted to hold the steering wheel tighter. 'We're going to be in for a rough ride. There'll be snow up at Kalb Pass.'

All of Philip's happiness faded away and, as the lorry began to twist and turn its way up the steep mountain road, he began to feel scared.

A few minutes later the snow began. At first it was a fine snow, like rain, but soon there were big flakes whizzing towards them and sticking on the windscreen. Jim turned the wipers on. They swished backwards and forwards, clearing the flakes, but the snow piled up and up at the bottom of the windscreen until the wipers could only move a little bit and it became impossible to see out.

'I've never seen snow like it. We'll have to stop,' Jim said, pulling to the side of the road and turning the engine off.

They stayed there for over two hours while the wind howled and the snow whirled and spun round them. Each time Jim wound the window down to look out, flakes of snow swirled in and melted on the floor. Once or twice Jim hummed a little tune and tapped his fingers on the steering wheel, but he didn't speak the whole time they waited.

At last, though, Jim opened the window and they found that the snow had stopped.

'Keep your fingers crossed,' Jim said as he started the engine. He turned the wheel and the lorry began to move slowly forward.

Philip crossed his fingers and peered out of the windscreen. There was so much snow that it was hard to see the road, and what made it worse was that on one side of them there was a steep drop down into the valley. Every so often the tyres started to spin on the steep hill and the lorry skidded sideways towards the edge but Jim kept the lorry going smoothly and bit by bit they climbed higher.

'Once more bend and we'll be at Kalb Pass,' Jim said. 'Then we'll be able to take it nice and easy down the other side.'

Philip watched as they crawled up towards the bend, and his fingers hurt from crossing them so hard. Jim turned the steering wheel and they were almost round the bend when the rear wheels began to spin on the slippery snow. The lorry jerked and slid towards the drop.

Philip grabbed hold of the door to steady himself then gasped with horror as it swung open. He found himself hanging half in and half out of the cab. The lorry was sliding nearer and nearer the edge and as Philip looked down he saw that he was dangling right over the drop.

He kicked his legs to try and drag himself back into the cab but it was no good. His arms were growing weak from holding the door and far, far below the sharp rocks were waiting for him to slip and fall.

Then he felt a hand grab hold of his ankle and the next second Jim pulled him back inside. At the same moment, the lorry skidded the other way on to the road again, and the door slammed shut.

'Phew, that was a close one,' Jim said. 'That door shouldn't have opened like that. I don't understand it.'

Philip sat back on the seat, shaking with fright. He couldn't understand how the door had come open either. He hadn't touched the handle. It was almost as if someone or something had opened it from outside. Nothing made any sense. Not the door, nor all this snow. How had this storm come so suddenly, out of nowhere? Philip had a nasty feeling that the Prince of Darkness was somewhere near and was trying to stop them from getting across the mountains. A couple of minutes later he was sure it was true.

Jim said, 'We're OK now – there's Kalb Pass ahead,' and he started to hum happily. Suddenly the humming stopped and he said, 'Oh no!'

Philip's heart sank as he looked out of the windscreen and saw the huge tree that was lying right across the road.

CHAPTER TWENTY

Jim stopped the lorry and they got out. Philip
looked round warily. He was certain now – the
Prince of Darkness was very near; the air was filled
with something evil and dangerous. He started to
follow Jim but then stopped to pull the rucksack
out of the lorry and put it on his back. He mustn't
leave Baby B and Nick on their own. Not here
where anything could happen.

Jim was standing next to the big pine tree when
Philip got up to him.

'Must have blown down in the storm,' Jim said.
'It looks as if we'll have to turn back. Unless, of
course . . .'

He walked towards the side of the road where
the tree had stood.

'Yes,' he said, 'there's just a chance that I could
drive the lorry up this little bank here and round

the end of the tree. It'll be a tight squeeze but . . .
Wait a minute, look at that!'

Philip looked where Jim was pointing and his
heart started to pound faster. There was a straight,
neat line across the tree trunk. The tree hadn't
been blown down – it had been sawn down.

'Now who would do a terrible thing like that?'
Jim whispered.

Philip didn't bother to reply, but he knew who
had done it. The Prince of Darkness.

He looked round him. Kalb Pass was a narrow
valley running between the high mountains. It was
a perfect place for a trap. He looked up and saw
the huge cliffs of snow and ice on the side of the
jagged mountain that towered above him.

'Well,' said Jim, 'I still think there's room for
us to drive the lorry round this tree. Give me a
hand to move some of these small branches then
we'll have a go.'

Jim began pulling at some of the branches and
twigs and Philip got hold of a large branch and
dragged it out of the way. He was just going to
pick up another one when he froze. The word,
'DANGER' flashed across his mind and then came
again – 'DANGER'.

Philip's eyes were looking at the branch he was
about to pick up but something clicked inside his
brain and he suddenly found himself looking down
from the top of the mountain. He could see the
lorry. He could see the tree lying across the road

with Jim standing next to it. And he could even see himself – a small figure bent over, looking at the branch. It was the strangest thing that had ever happened to him but he didn't have time to think about it because he had also seen something else.

Halfway down the mountain, a huge black shape was standing at the top of one of the ice cliffs. Philip saw the black shape start to push the ice, and he knew what was going to happen. At any second now, thousands of tons of ice and snow would slide off the mountain and crash down into Kalb Pass.

His brain clicked again and he found himself back on the ground, looking at the branch. He stood up and shouted, 'Avalanche! Run!'

Out of the corner of his eye he saw Jim straighten up and start to run towards the lorry. At the same moment there was a loud crack from up above and Philip turned and started to run in the other direction, away from the lorry.

As he ran, he began to count. One. Two. Three. Four. There was another loud crack and the air was filled with a shivering, hissing roar. He kept running – away from all that ice and snow falling down towards him. Five, Six, Seven, Eight . . . Run . . . Keep running . . . Nine . . . Ten . . .

There was a booming CRUMP! and a second later Philip felt himself hit by a wave of air that lifted him up and threw him forward. He crashed to the ground and lumps of ice beat down all round him.

The tinkling, pattering sound of the falling ice finally stopped and Philip got up. A huge wall of snow now stretched from one side of the narrow valley to the other. Kalb Pass was completely blocked. The pine tree lay hidden under tons and tons of snow and Philip felt weak when he thought of how he had been standing next to it only a few seconds ago.

But where was Jim. Had he been crushed under all that?

'Jim! Jim!' he yelled.

There was silence.

He was just about to call again when there was a cry and he saw the farmer scramble up from the other side and stand on the top of the white wall.

'Thank heavens you're safe,' Jim shouted. 'If it hadn't been for you, we'd both be under this lot. How did you know it was going to fall?'

'I just guessed,' Philip called, knowing that he would never be able to explain it all.

'Well, anyway, we'll never get the lorry past all this,' Jim said, 'so you'd better climb up here and we'll go back.'

Philip thought for a moment, then shook his head. 'Thanks, Jim, but I must go on. I've got to get somewhere quickly. You go back.'

'Are you sure?' Jim called.

'Yes. It's all downhill now. Thanks for the lift.'

'OK, lad, but look after yourself. And thank you – without you, I'd be buried under all this. Bye.'

'Bye. Give my love to Birdie when you see her.'

'I will, lad. Good luck.'

Philip waved then turned and began walking down the road. He had only gone a couple of paces when there was a whisper from inside the rucksack. It was Baby B.

'Flipip, Flipip – what happened? Me and Nick is millions bumpered up and down.'

Philip glanced over his shoulder and saw Jim still waving to him, so he waved back and whispered, 'We've just had a narrow escape. It was the Prince of Darkness. I'll tell you all about it later but I want to get right away from Kalb Pass before he tries anything else.'

CHAPTER TWENTY-ONE

Philip ran all the way along the narrow valley, looking up at the mountains in case the Prince of Darkness sent more snow crashing down. Then, at last, he reached the end of Kalb Pass and came out into the bright sunshine. He felt much safer there, but he kept going until he saw a small stone cottage by the side of the road.

All the windows were boarded up and when Philip tried the big wooden door it was locked. It was obvious that nobody lived there during the winter, so he took off the rucksack and lifted Baby B and Nick out. They ran around to stretch themselves a bit while Philip looked for somewhere to sit.

He found a large, thick plastic sack at the side of the house and he put it on the snow and sat down with his back against the wall. He got some of Birdie's sandwiches out and when Baby B and

Nick came back they all sat in the warm sun to eat them. And while they ate, Philip told them the whole story.

When he got to the bit about how he had suddenly seen everything from the top of the mountain, Baby B said, 'Coo, Flipip, you can do magic ever so good now – just like Grandpa Edgar.'

At the end of the story Baby B and Nick wanted to build a snowman, and while they messed around Philip looked at the map. Once they got to the bottom of the mountains they would have about ten miles to walk before they came to Tarika Head.

He stared away into the distance. They were very, very high here. The snow stretched away down the slope for miles and miles and then, beyond that, he could just make out the green where the fields must begin. Well, they ought to get going at once. The sun was already beginning to sink low and there were some more black clouds on the horizon. It would be awful to be caught up here by the dark and more snow.

As he stood up and put the rucksack on, he trod on the plastic sack and it skidded away across the snow. At once he had an idea and he called to Baby B and Nick.

'Listen, you two. I've thought of a way to get down the mountain quickly.'

'I know, I can do my rolling,' said Nick, and he started to curl up into a ball.

'No, no – don't do that, Nick,' Philip shouted.

'Once you start rolling you'll pick up more and more snow until you become a huge snowball rolling down the hill.'

The idea of Nick in the middle of a huge snowball struck Baby B as very funny and he fell about laughing. By the time he had finished he was so covered in snow that he looked a bit like a snowball himself.

'Come on,' Philip chuckled, brushing the snow off Baby B, 'let's get going.' He sat down on the plastic sack and told Baby B and Nick to sit down behind him. Then he lifted the front of the sack so that it curved up like the front of a sledge.

'Hold tight!' he called, then bounced up and down a couple of times. The plastic sack slid forward and in no time at all they were whizzing down the slope.

'Wheeeeee!' shrieked Baby B and Nick, and Philip felt them grab on to the back of his anorak to stop themselves from falling off.

They sped faster and faster down the slope, laughing and giggling and shouting, 'Whoopee!' as the sparkling snow sprayed up all round them.

'It's millions lovely,' Baby B shouted and then added, 'Whoops!' as they hit a bump and flew into the air.

'Oooof!' they all gasped as the sack swished down on to the soft snow again and raced on faster than ever.

Philip found that he could steer by pulling the

front of the plastic to the left or to the right, so when they came to a dark green pine wood he was able to guide the sack on to a path that ran through the trees. They zipped along the path, twisting and turning to avoid bushes and trees, and then, with a WHOOSH, they burst out on to the wide snowfields again.

For another ten minutes they raced downhill, skimming across the snow so fast that it was like flying. Then, suddenly, they were at the bottom. The sack slid off the snow on to grass and jolted to a halt. Philip got up and looked back to the top of the mountain. It was miles away. They had made really good time – and it was just as well, because it was growing dark and the clouds had covered the setting sun. A thin drizzle was starting to fall.

'Sliding is even nicer than rolling,' Nick said, coming to stand next to Philip. 'I want to do another one.'

'Oh yes, Flipip, can we do another one?' Baby B asked.

'I'm afraid we haven't got time,' Philip said. 'We've got to find somewhere to spend the night before the weather gets worse. Come on.'

Baby B and Nick walked for a while but they did such a lot of chasing around that they soon got tired and wanted to ride in the rucksack. They were quite heavy to carry but Philip was pleased because he could go faster like that.

It really was getting darker every minute and the drizzle was turning to rain. The sooner they found themselves somewhere to stay, the happier he would be. He certainly didn't want to have to walk at night with the Prince of Darkness around.

He was just beginning to get really worried when he saw a small barn at the edge of a field. He swung the door open. A farmer had used it to store his hay and it was dry and sweet-smelling. They sat on one of the hay bales and looked out of the door while they finished off the last of the sandwiches and ate the apples that Birdie had given them.

It was good to be somewhere warm and dry, and they stared out of the door at the grey rain pouring down, making the distant trees pale and misty. Then, as the night closed in, Baby B and Nick sang their song.

Run to Beaver Towers. Run to Beaver Towers.
Through the wind and through the showers.
It might take us hours and hours
Before we're back at Beaver Towers.
But it's run to Beaver Towers.
Yes, run to Beaver Towers.
Past the trees and past the flowers.
Flipip's using all his powers
To take us back to Beaver Towers.

When it was dark-blue night outside and they couldn't see things any more, they closed the door

and made themselves a bed in a soft pile of hay.
They snuggled close to each other and were as
warm as toast. They hummed the song gently and
soon fell asleep.

CHAPTER TWENTY-TWO

They were up and on the road as soon as the day began to dawn. Philip's breath steamed in the cold air and the hedgerows were filled with frost-covered cobwebs that sparkled in the fresh light. Baby B kept finding bits of hay that had got stuck in Nick's prickles during the night and they both tried chewing some of it because they were so hungry.

Then, while they were walking through a wood, they found some real food – chestnuts. Baby B was very good at tearing off the shells with his sharp front teeth and soon there was a big pile of them, peeled and ready to eat. The chestnuts were crisp and crunchy and sweet and delicious and by the time they set off again their tummies were full.

Baby B and Nick had lots of energy after their breakfast and they managed to walk for nearly three miles before their short legs became too tired to go on. Philip popped them into the rucksack and, while they sang the song over and over again, he walked on as fast as he could. The rucksack was heavy, though, and every couple of miles he had to sit down to rest his aching back and sore feet.

Then, at last, as he was crossing a field, he smelt a salty tang in the air and a few minutes later he was standing at the top of a cliff looking down at the shimmering sea. They had made it. They were at Tarika Head. Somewhere, hundreds of miles away across all that shining water, were the two islands and Beaver Towers.

He sat down and let Baby B and Nick out of the rucksack. They were full of beans again and began trying to jump higher than each other to see if they could catch a glimpse of Beaver Towers. Philip explained that it was still a long way away and that they would have to be patient because it would probably take ages for the kite and the cloud to come.

Then Baby B said that he wanted to go down and swim in the sea, and Nick said he wanted to do some rolling down the hills. Finally Philip managed to persuade them to go off across the fields to collect things to eat and he made them promise not to go near the edge of the cliffs. They ran off, pleased to have an important job to do, and Philip settled down to try to call the dragon kite and the cloud.

He didn't really know how he was supposed to do it, so he just closed his eyes, tried to get a clear picture of them in his mind, and then said, over and over again, 'Come to Tarika Head.'

Supposing they hadn't heard? He stood up and, just in case, filled his lungs and shouted with all his might, 'Please cloud! Please dragon kite! Come to Tarika Head as quickly as you can.'

Even though it was his loudest shout, it sounded very feeble and the words seemed to fade away into all the huge space in front of him. Oh dear, supposing it didn't work? He sat down and tried not to be worried and afraid.

He was still sitting there, nearly an hour later, staring anxiously at the horizon, when Baby B and Nick came back. Baby B's dungarees were filthy dirty and Nick had pieces of leaves and grass stuck to his prickles but they proudly showed him a pile of mushrooms and acorns they had collected. Philip told them they had done a very good job and they beamed with happiness and then began to eat. Philip didn't feel very hungry, but he slowly nibbled a couple of mushrooms and said how tasty they were.

'The acorns is bestest,' Baby B said, holding out a pawful of them for Philip.

'Thanks, Baby B, but human beings don't eat those.'

'Coo, I'm glad I'm not a human beak, aren't you, Nick?'

'Yes,' said Nick, 'acorns is lovely.' The little hedgehog put another one in his mouth and when he had finished munching it he asked, 'Where is the cloud and the kite, Flipip?'

'Oh Nick,' Baby B said, 'Flipip said we got to be playshent, didn't you, Flipip?'

Philip nodded.

'Flipip?' Baby B asked. 'What does it mean, playshent?'

'Being patient means you just have to wait for things,' he said.

'See, Nick – we got to wait,' Baby B said.

And they waited and waited and waited and waited. Hours went by. Baby B and Nick got bored sitting there so they ran around and played. Then they got bored with that and came back and curled up and had a sleep.

'Is we still waiting?' Baby B asked when he woke up.

'Yes. Not long now, I hope,' Philip said, trying to sound cheerful. He knew that it would take the cloud and the kite ages to make the journey but he still couldn't stop worrying. Perhaps it would be better if he could get closer to the islands and try to call again.

At that very moment he caught sight of a small fishing boat chugging out to sea. He got up and looked over the cliff. There, just below Tarika Head, was a tiny fishing village with steep, narrow streets and white stone cottages leading down to a little harbour. Six brightly-coloured fishing boats were bobbing up and down on the water inside the harbour walls.

It took only a moment for Philip to make up his mind. He put Baby B and Nick into the rucksack, swung it on to his back and set off down the cliff path to the village. If, somehow, he could get on board one of those boats it might take him far enough out to sea to make the difference when he called the cloud and kite again.

There was a small church at the top of the village and he was just passing the churchyard gate when he heard a loud voice, singing a hymn. He turned to look and saw a man come out of the shadows at the side of the church. He was a tall man with whiskers all over his face and an old sailor's cap on his head. The man strolled to the gate, still singing the hymn, then he stopped and smiled at Philip.

'Hello, young lad,' he said in a loud, cheerful voice. Then he winked. 'You dodged off school for the afternoon, then?'

Philip shook his head.

'On holiday, perhaps?'

Philip didn't say anything.

'Going down to the harbour to look at the boats, I'll be bound. Eh? Yes, I thought as much – I always used to do that when I was a lad. Mind if I join you on the stroll down?'

Philip shook his head and they set off together

down the steep, narrow lane, with the man whistling the hymn.

'Well, here we are,' the man said as they turned a corner and came out on to the side of the harbour. 'Don't those boats look a pretty sight? And the prettiest of them all is that red one, there – don't you think so?'

'Yes, it's lovely,' Philip said.

'Good, I'm glad you like her – she's mine. Yes, the prettiest and the fastest and the safest little tub that sails these waters, she is. Well, I'll bid you good day – I'm just off to do some lobstering. Enjoy your look round.'

Philip thanked the man and watched him as he walked along the harbour wall. The man was just about to jump on board his boat when he turned and called, 'Hey, lad, I don't suppose you'd like a little sea trip, would you? You could give me a hand with the pots. We wouldn't be more than a couple of hours – you'd be back in time for tea.'

Philip could hardly believe his ears. What a piece of luck! He ran up to the boat and said, 'Oh, yes, please. I'd love it.'

'Well then – welcome aboard,' said the man, and he put his arm round Philip's shoulder and they stepped on to the boat. 'My name's Captain Nomed. What's yours?'

'Philip.'

'Right then, Philip – let's cast off.'

Captain Nomed started the engine then undid

the rope that tied them to the wall and the boat headed out of the harbour. As they left the harbour, the boat hit the waves of the open sea and began to rock up and down.

Philip grabbed on to the boat's side and went pale, but it wasn't the waves that had made him feel sick and weak. Just as they had passed the lighthouse that marked the end of the harbour, he had heard a voice inside his head. Somehow, he had managed to overhear what the Captain was thinking.

And the words that he had heard were, 'Good. Now I've got them.'

CHAPTER TWENTY-THREE

Philip didn't know what to do. He held on to the side of the boat and looked at the land getting further and further away. Already it was too late to call for help. They were trapped.

There was a tap on his shoulder and he jumped in fright. Captain Nomed was standing next to him. There was a big, cheerful smile on his whiskery face.

'What's the matter with you, lad? Feeling a bit seasick? Don't worry, you just stay there a while until you get your sea legs. I'll get the pots ready and you can give me a hand when you feel up to it.'

The Captain smiled again and went to the front of the boat. He bent down to sort out the lobster pots and started to sing the hymn. His deep, tuneful voice sounded so jolly, and his smile had been so kind and friendly. Perhaps it was all a silly mistake – he seemed such a nice man. Perhaps Philip hadn't heard his thoughts at all. Just because he knew there was such a thing as think-talking didn't mean that he could know what everyone was thinking.

The little boat hit a wave and the wind blew some salty spray into Philip's face. The fresh, cold tingle on his cheeks seemed to snap him out of his fears. No, there was nothing horrible about Captain Nomed. And the further they went out to sea, the closer they would be to Beaver Towers. He would wait a bit longer and then he would try calling the cloud and the kite again. Meanwhile, he would take the rucksack off and go and help the Captain with pots.

'Aha, feeling better already. I knew you'd soon get used to it,' the Captain said as Philip joined him. 'Well, now you can earn your keep by carting these pots down to the stern ready for dropping over. Mind how you go – it's getting a bit choppy.'

It was true – the sea was getting much rougher now, but Philip liked the feel of the boat bouncing up and down and it was fun trying to walk straight as he carried the pots across the rocking deck. As he worked, he found himself singing the same hymn that the Captain was singing and the bright, bouncy tune seemed to fit the movement of the boat.

Every now and then Philip glanced at the sky to check whether there was any sign of the cloud and the kite. Both times they had carried him across the sea it had taken all night but they could probably go much faster when they weren't carrying him. It must be about six hours since he had called them. If they had heard him, they must be nearly here – yet, each time he looked, the sky was empty. Perhaps he should try again. He closed his eyes and tried to think really hard.

It was funny, though – he just couldn't get a clear picture of them. Instead, it was like listening to a radio that wasn't properly tuned. A number of different voices were talking and the sounds were all jumbled up. Philip tried to listen to what they were saying.

'Do it . . . The Captain is . . . Now . . . Back to . . . Yes, Master . . . Front.' The words were all muddled up and didn't make any sense. Philip opened his eyes and the voices stopped.

How strange. There had been three voices. One was very deep and growly. The second one sounded like a man who was scared. And the third – the third had sounded a bit like Mr Edgar.

He closed his eyes again and this time he heard the words 'Back to front' very clearly, and he was sure it was Mr Edgar's voice.

Back to front? What was back to front? It was all so odd that Philip felt as if *he* was back to front. He opened his eyes. He must stop all this thinking – he was getting as muddled up as the words. He walked across the swaying deck and Captain

Nomed turned and smiled and winked at him as he picked up another pot.

But even as he went on working, Philip couldn't stop wondering what 'Back to front' meant. What were the other words he had heard? 'Do it.' Do it back to front? It couldn't be that. 'Now.' 'Yes, Master.' That didn't fit. 'The Captain.' The Captain is back to front? How could Captain Nomed be back to front?

Captain.

Nomed. Nomed.

Philip dropped the lobster pot in fright. Nomed back to front. DEMON.

And suddenly he knew the three things that had been said.

'The captain is back to front.' That had been Mr Edgar.

'Do it now.' That had been the deep growly voice of the Prince of Darkness.

'Yes, Master.' That had been Captain Nomed. Captain Nomed the Demon.

Something flashed past Philip's eyes and before he had time to move he felt a rope tighten round him, pinning his arms to his sides. He was jerked round and came face to face with Captain Nomed.

'Well, well,' sneered the Captain, and all the smiles had gone, leaving him looking ugly and cruel. 'Look who's fallen right into a trap.'

CHAPTER TWENTY-FOUR

Captain Nomed wound the rope round Philip another three times then roughly pushed him to the deck and tied his feet together.

'Now I've got you where I want you,' hissed the Captain. 'And if it was up to me I'd throw you overboard right now and let you die in the sea – the very place you killed my sister.'

'Oyin was your sister?' Philip gasped, hardly daring to look at those wicked eyes that stared down at him with such hatred.

'Yes, my dear, dear sister. And you killed her. How I'd love to watch you struggle and sink like she did. Unfortunately, my master has other plans for you.'

'Your master? The Prince of Darkness?'

'The very same. My master, the ruler of the World of Shadows and soon the ruler of this world, too. And guess what, little man – you are going to help him win this world. You may be no more than a little shrimp but we know that you've started to develop the Power. Very useful that, the Power. No end to the kind of things you could do. Yes, my master is going to find you very useful.'

'I'll never help him,' Philip shouted, struggling to get free of the rope.

'Won't you? Oh, won't you?' laughed Captain Nomed. 'My master will soon change your mind when he gets hold of you. He's waiting on an island not far from here – we'll be there soon. But in the mean time I might change your mind myself. He'll be pleased with me if I save him the trouble.'

The Captain spun round and went over to the rucksack. He undid the flaps, plunged his hands inside, and pulled out Baby B and Nick. They looked helplessly towards Philip, but even before they had a chance to call to him, the Captain opened one of the lobster pots and dropped them inside. He closed the pot and tied a rope to the handle.

'Perhaps this will change your mind,' Captain Nomed said, coming towards Philip, swinging the pot at the end of the rope. 'If you don't agree to help the Prince of Darkness, I'll drop these two animals over the side. There are some hungry lobsters down there who would find them very, very tasty. It's up to you. All you have to do is say, Yes, and your two friends can go free. If not, say goodbye to them for ever.'

Philip looked at Baby B and Nick and they looked back at him through the wooden bars of the lobster pot.

'Yes' was such a little word to say, and it would save Baby B and Nick. But 'Yes' was the word that Oyin had wanted him to say when she had tried to trick him in the library. If he had said 'Yes' then, she would have captured the whole of Beaver Towers. If he said 'Yes' now, he might help the Prince of Darkness to win the whole world. Philip gulped. He couldn't say 'Yes', but if he said 'No' he would be killing his two dearest friends.

'Flipip,' Baby B said in a scared voice.

Philip looked at him and felt the tears come to his eyes. He shook his head in misery and, leaning forward, he said quietly, 'Oh, Baby B, what can I do?'

Baby B poked his paw through the bars and touched the side of Philip's face. 'Tell him "No", Flipip. Me and Nick want you to tell him "No", don't we, Nick?'

The little hedgehog opened his mouth to speak but he was so scared that he couldn't make a sound. Instead he nodded his head.

'I see,' roared Captain Nomed. 'You two feel brave, do you? Well, a couple of minutes dangling in the water will soon cure you of that.'

He swung the pot over the side of the boat and tied the rope to a piece of metal.

'There,' Captain Nomed said, turning back to Philip with a horrible grin on his face. 'They're nearly underwater. You should see them struggling around in the pot trying to keep their heads in the air – it's really funny. I'll pull them out in a couple of minutes and give you another chance.'

At that moment the boat hit a big wave and bucked into the air.

'Getting rougher,' chuckled the Captain. 'These waves will soon finish those two off and I won't have time to pull them out now because I'm going to be too busy steering the boat to where my master is waiting. So say goodbye to your friends.'

He laughed and walked towards the steering wheel at the front of the boat. He swung the wheel and they changed direction and began to hit bigger and bigger waves.

As the boat heaved up and down, Philip rolled around helplessly on the deck. Then, as he came to rest on his back, he saw something that made his heart leap.

CHAPTER TWENTY-FIVE

Philip lay on the deck and blinked his eyes to make sure that he hadn't made a mistake. No, it wasn't a mistake. There, racing across the sky, was the little round cloud and just behind it was the huge dragon kite with its long tail fluttering in the wind. They were heading straight for the boat, coming lower and lower. At any moment Captain Nomed might see them.

Philip silently gave them an order. 'No, don't come down yet. Go higher in the sky and wait for me to call.'

At once the cloud and the kite soared high into the sky and began circling round, waiting to be called. Philip's heart was beating fast. He had done it. He could make them do what he wanted, just by thinking. But, no matter how hard he thought, he wouldn't be able to make them do things that they couldn't do. They couldn't cut his ropes, for example; and they couldn't rescue poor Baby B and Nick.

Oh, if only he could get free.

He pulled and pulled at the ropes but it was no good, the knots just got tighter.

It was silly to waste time and energy like that – he must lie still and try to think clearly. As soon as he did, he realized that he had been looking at the problem the wrong way. If he couldn't free himself to rescue Baby B and Nick, then they had to free themselves to rescue him.

Baby B had said that he and Nick had tried to do think-talking and had nearly managed to do it. Baby B had been boasting, of course, but perhaps it was true, and perhaps the little beaver had improved the same way he had improved. Anyway, it was their only hope. It had to work. It had to.

Philip closed his eyes and thought with all his might. 'Baby B,' he thought. 'Baby B – can you hear me? It's Philip.'

There was a loud shout of surprise inside Philip's head. 'Flipip. It's me, Baby B. Help! Help! Where is you?'

'Ssh! Ssh!' Philip thought. 'We're doing think-talking, Baby B.'

'No, Flipip. I can't do think-talking – I can only try but I isn't very good to do it.'

'You can, you can.' Philip thought, as strongly as he could. 'We are doing it now. And you must listen carefully, Baby B, very carefully because we haven't got a moment to lose.'

There was a loud scream inside Philip's head and then a jumble of words – 'Look out. Wave . . . Oh help . . . Nick . . . Nick.'

The boat rocked violently and Philip knew what had happened. A big wave had hit them.

'Baby B. Baby B, are you all right?' Philip thought.

There was a long pause and then he heard Baby B's think-talking voice say, 'Ouch, that hurts.'

'Are you all right? Baby B, answer me.'

'I is all right?' Baby B said, 'but Nick is sitting on my head and he is prickerling me.'

Philip almost had to laugh but he thought hard and said, 'Now, listen carefully. Do you think your teeth are strong enough to bite through the lobster pot?'

'Yes it's easy. I can chop down little trees even. But if I make a hole we will fall in the sea and the lobsterers will eat us all up.'

'No you won't,' Philip said. 'I want you to bite a hole near the top and then climb up the rope into the boat. Then I want Nick to run and hide in the rucksack and I want you to come and bite through my ropes. But you must be very careful because Captain Nomed mustn't see you. Do you understand?'

'Yes, but Nick can't climb the rope, Flipip, his paws is too little to hold on.'

'Well, you must let him hang on to the back of your dungarees and you'll have to climb up with him. He'll be heavy but you've got to do it. Hurry. Hurry!'

'All right,' Baby B said.

Philip caught some of the words as Baby B whispered to Nick then there was a loud crunching noise inside his head. He was hearing the sounds of Baby B biting through the lobster pot.

'Easy peasy,' Baby B said. 'Flipip, I done it – I made a big hole. Now I'm going to climb the rope. Ooops, it's millions wet and slippery.'

'Be careful,' Philip said, then looked towards where the rope came over the side of the boat and was tied to the piece of metal. In a minute, if all went well, he would see Baby B's head come over the top.

'I'm doing it,' Baby B said. 'It's millions slidey and Nick is a bit millions heavy but . . . Oh no . . . Look out . . . A wave!'

Even from where he was lying on the deck, Philip could see the huge, grey-green wave sweeping in towards the boat. It smashed against the side and, as spray flew everywhere, he heard Baby B scream. The boat tipped sideways as it rode up the wave and then tipped the other way as it slid down the other side.

'Baby B,' he called.

There was no sound.

CHAPTER TWENTY-SIX

Philip was so worried that he almost called out loud, but he made himself think-talk again. 'Baby B! Oh, Baby B, please answer. Where are you?'

'Blurggh, I is all soaking,' came Baby B's voice. 'But we is nearly at the top.'

A moment later Philip almost cheered as he saw Baby B's wet head poke over the side of the boat. The little beaver hauled himself over the edge and jumped lightly on to the deck. Philip glanced towards the front of the boat. The Captain had his back to them and was holding tightly to the wheel, trying to steer the boat through the waves.

'Quick,' Philip thought. 'Baby B to me and Nick to the rucksack.'

Nick moved first. He let go of the dungarees, bumped to the deck and dashed to the rucksack. Luckily it was lying on its side and Philip saw him dart in and disappear from view. Now it was Baby

B's turn. He would have to run across the whole width of the deck and if Captain Nomed happened to turn round he would be seen at once. Well, there was no point in waiting – they would just have to hope.

'Now,' Philip thought, and Baby B came racing towards him. There was a pool of water on the deck where the wave had splashed over and, before Philip could warn him, Baby B's feet skidded into it. He lost his balance and fell with a loud bump.

Philip looked anxiously towards the Captain but he didn't move and a second later Baby B was up and running again. He sped to Philip's side and sat down out of sight of the Captain.

'I bonked my nose,' he said out loud, and then put his paw to his mouth when he realized what he'd done.

'Ssh!' Philip thought.

'Sorry,' Baby B thought. 'Oh, Flipip, isn't it good? I can do think-talking as good as anything. Grandpa Edgar will be ever so pleased.'

'Baby B, ssh!' Philip thought. 'We haven't got time to waste. Try and bite through my ropes quickly.'

Baby B disappeared behind his back and Philip felt the rope move as the little beaver's teeth began to gnaw at it.

'Blurggh, it tastes smelly!' Baby B thought, and Philip couldn't help smiling.

It seemed to take ages and Philip kept glancing

at Captain Nomed, but he was so busy with the wheel that he didn't look round once. Then, at last, he felt the rope go loose and he heard Baby B's thought, 'Hooray, I bited it all in pieces.'

'Well done,' Philip thought. 'Now quickly – run to the rucksack and get inside. As soon as I've untied my feet I'll come and put it on my back. The cloud and the dragon kite are waiting for us up in the sky. I'll call them down and we'll fly off this boat and leave that demon, Nomed, behind. Quick, off you go.'

Baby B ran to the rucksack and dived inside and Philip began untying the rope around his feet. The knot was tight and his fingers kept slipping but he finally got it undone.

Very slowly and carefully, he stood up and began to tiptoe towards the rucksack. He bent down and started to do up the flap. He looked up at the sky and saw the cloud and the dragon kite high above, circling round and round.

'Now, Cloud; now Kite,' he thought, as he finished fastening the flap, 'dive down as quickly as you can and pick us up.'

He stood up and got ready to put the rucksack on his back. Out of the corner of his eye he saw Captain Nomed turn and glance towards him. The Captain gave a terrible roar and swung round, letting the wheel of the boat spin wildly.

At once, the waves caught the boat and sent it rocking more than ever. Philip felt his feet slip away as the boat tilted to one side and he crashed down on to the deck. As he lay there, trying to get his breath back, he could see the big boots of the Captain racing towards him. He staggered to his feet and dodged aside as the Captain made a grab for him.

Again the boat bucked and jumped as another wave hit it and Philip found himself thrown up against the front of the little cabin. His head bumped against the wood and stars exploded in front of his eyes. He blinked and saw Captain Nomed charging towards him so he scrambled past the side of the cabin to the very front of the boat.

It was only when he got there and skidded to a halt at the edge of the deck that he realized he had made a mistake. There was nowhere else to run to. Just below him the sharp prow of the boat was slicing its way through the huge waves. He turned. Captain Nomed was there, blocking his way back to safety.

'So,' said the Captain, opening his mouth in an evil grin that showed his teeth that suddenly looked pointed and sharp. 'So, you thought you'd get away, did you?'

The Captain took a step forwards and Philip took a step backwards. He could feel his feet right on the edge of the deck. The boat dipped down one wave and Philip almost tumbled backwards but then it started to rise up another wave and he managed to get his balance.

'I should let you fall,' Captain Nomed hissed. 'Let you fall into all that terrible water like you did to my sister, Oyin.'

The boat was still rising up the wave and now Philip could see behind the Captain's head. The cloud and the dragon kite were rushing towards the boat. An idea flashed into Philip's brain and he gave them an order – 'Dive. Dive. To me. To me.'

Then, out loud, he said to the Captain, 'Come and get me. Or are you scared of the water like your horrible sister? I tricked her and she was melted by the sea. There was nothing left but bones.'

'You little cheat,' snarled the Captain. 'You killed her. But you'll be sorry to hear that water can't melt me.'

They were coming. The cloud and the kite were coming.

'Try and get me, then,' Philip shouted. 'Just think what the Prince of Darkness will do to you if I throw myself in the water.'

'Oh no you don't,' yelled the Captain and he made a grab for Philip.

Philip dodged to one side and as the Captain sprang forward the cloud whizzed by his head. He stopped in surprise, his feet on the very edge of the deck. At the next instant, the kite shot by, clipping him on the back of his head. He toppled, screaming, into the sea. There was a loud thump as the front of the boat hit him and he disappeared under the waves.

Philip knew there was no time to lose. It wouldn't be long before the Prince of Darkness found out that his demon was dead. He ran along the deck, swung the rucksack on to his back, and called the cloud and the kite.

They came skimming in low across the sea and stopped just above his head. He reached up, took hold of the kite, and a second later he felt himself lifted into the air. They climbed quickly, higher and higher, then glided round and headed towards the setting sun.

They were going back to Beaver Towers.

CHAPTER TWENTY-SEVEN

They flew all night and Philip didn't close his eyes once, just in case the Prince of Darkness tried to follow them. Then, as the sun rose, he saw the islands ahead of them.

As they flew over Round Rock Island the cloud and the kite started to dive, and by the time they reached the big island they were skimming just above the tree tops. When Beaver Towers came in sight, Philip was amazed to see flags flying from the turrets of the castle and all the animals standing on the top of the walls, waving and shouting.

There was a big cheer as they landed in the courtyard. Philip let go of the kite and it went flying off with the cloud. Almost before he had time to take the rucksack off, all the animals had run down from the castle walls and were crowding round, laughing and shouting and patting him on the back. There was an extra special loud cheer as he lifted up the flap of the rucksack and Baby B and Nick popped up to say hello.

'Hold your horses, everybody, hold your horses!' came Mr Edgar's voice from the back of the crowd. The animals stood aside and the old beaver came forward slowly with a big smile on his face.

He took hold of Philip's hand and winked. 'Well done, young 'un, well done. I'm proud of you. Now then, everybody, these three young heroes look as if they are hungry and tired. I suggest we let them get their breath back and we can hear all about their adventures later. We'll have a big party this evening, with singing and dancing and plenty of lovely food for everyone.'

All the animals cheered and went off to their jobs talking about the fun they were going to have that evening.

Philip, Baby B and Nick followed Mr Edgar into the castle kitchen and there was Mrs Badger. She gave Philip and Baby B a big hug and kissed Nick on his snout because he was a bit too prickly to hug, then she sat them down at the table and served a huge breakfast. They were very hungry and they ate it all up.

'Now,' said Mr Edgar, as they finished, 'I think Baby B ought to pop off and see his mummy and daddy. And Nick, you'd better nip off and find Mick and Ann – the Mechanics aren't the same without you and I'm sure that old car, Doris, has missed your polishing.'

Baby B and Nick ran off together and Mr Edgar turned to Philip. 'Well, young 'un, I think we'll go up to the library – we've got some important things to talk about.'

It was strange for Philip to sit down in front of the library fire and look across at Mr Edgar, just as he had when they had been doing the think-talking on Drevish Moor. They sat silently for a while, staring at the flickering flames of the fire, then Philip began talking. He told the whole story from beginning to end and Mr Edgar listened without saying a word except when Philip got to the bit about how Baby B had done think-talking. Then he clapped his paws together and cried, 'Did he, now? Good, good! That's going to make things a lot easier.'

When Philip finished the story, Mr Edgar got up and walked slowly round the library, stroking his grey whiskers, deep in thought.

'Well,' he said, coming back and standing in front of the fire, 'that's quite a story, young 'un. Of course, you did a couple of madcap things like going out in old demon Nomed's boat – there was no need to try and get closer to call the cloud and the kite, they'd heard you all right.'

'But I didn't know if my power was strong enough, Mr Edgar.'

'No, of course, you didn't. But you know it now, don't you? It's getting stronger all the time – look at how you managed to hear my warning about old back to front Nomed. You did that on your own, because, as I told you, all my power is gone. And now we come to the point of why I wanted you back here.'

Mr Edgar's face became serious and he sat down and leaned across and talked slowly and quietly. It was as though Philip was seeing a new side of Mr Edgar that he'd never seen before.

'You're a special lad, Philip, and I've got something important to ask you. I want you to take over from me.'

Philip gulped. 'What do you mean?'

'What I say. I don't just mean looking after Beaver Towers. I mean using your power to fight all the evil work the Prince of Darkness tries to do in the world. You see, without all the animals and human beings who use their power to do good, that wicked beast would take over everything.'

'Are there many human beings who have got the power?' Philip asked.

'Oh, quite a few, yes. There should be lots more, of course, because all human beings have got it hidden inside them, but they're not ready to use it properly – so they can't use it. There are more animals who can do it because, although we're not as clever as humans, we're not as likely to do evil things. If only humans would wake up. They think they understand everything but they're a bit like a bird when it's still inside the egg. The little bird thinks his egg is the whole world until he chips his way out and finds a much bigger and more beautiful world outside. When humans chip their way out of their shells, they'll find that nearly all the things they believe are wrong.'

'I don't understand, Mr Edgar. What sort of things?'

'Well, let me give you an example, young 'un. It seems to you as if I'm standing still, doesn't it.'

Philip nodded.

'Aha – that's just where you're wrong,' Mr Edgar chuckled. 'I'm moving at a terrific speed because the earth is whizzing round in space. But to us, the earth *seems* as if it never moves. And there are lots of things that seem to be one thing but are really not like that at all. And those of us who know a bit more about these things have got to keep the world safe until everybody is ready to learn about them. So, what do you say – are you going to help?'

'What will I have to do?'

'I want you to come with me to visit some people and animals I know. They'll help you to learn things, mostly things about yourself. Because, don't forget, you can only learn about the power when you are ready. That's why you only started to do think-talking after you had found out how to be brave and think about others first.'

'But I won't have time,' Philip burst out. 'I've got to go home and see my parents.'

'Now don't you worry your head about that.

Time is one of those things I've been telling you about that only *seems* to be like it is. When you find out what it really is, you can pop backwards and forwards in it as easy as winking your eye. You'll be able to go back home and your mother and father won't even know you've been out of the house.'

Just at that moment there was the sound of excited voices and the noise of someone running up the stairs.

'Blow me down,' Mr Edgar said. 'What's all that? It sounds as if we've got visitors.'

CHAPTER TWENTY-EIGHT

The footsteps pounded along the corridor then the door burst open and Baby B and Nick raced into the room. Baby B skidded on one of the rugs, fell over, and slid across the polished floor until he bumped into Mr Edgar's legs and came to a stop.

'Now then, you young ruffian, what's all this hullaballoo?' Mr Edgar said, picking him up and dusting him down.

'Grandpa, Grandpa, you'll never guess what. Me and Nick can doing think-talking, can't we, Nick? We did doing it a bit with Flipip on the boat but now me and Nick can do it all by ourself. Nick was doing polishing the car with Ann and Mick and I wasn't there because I was in my room but we did it just like that. And it wasn't pretend and saying fibbers, it was real, wasn't it, Nick?'

Mr Edgar smiled and bent down and lifted Baby B in his arms. 'Yes, I know,' he said, giving his grandson a kiss on the cheek, 'Philip has told me all about it. And you know why you can do it? Because you were both very brave when that dratted old demon, Nomed, said he was going to feed you to the lobsters. I'm as pleased as Punch with both of you. Now, what do you all say to a bit of fresh air before this party begins.'

They strolled for hours in the woods round Beaver Towers. The sun was shining and the golden leaves on the ground made a crunching noise as they walked along, talking. Baby B kept them all in fits of laughter as he acted out all the exciting and scaring things that had happened to them on their adventures. He pretended to be Megs when she had barked at them in the kitchen, and he pretended to be the vet and Captain Nomed and all the people they had met on the journey.

By the time they went back into the castle, all the animals had finished their work for the day and were getting ready for the party. Baby B and Nick tried to help by blowing up balloons but they kept bursting on Nick's prickles so they worked at laying the tables instead.

Philip went into the kitchen and helped to prepare the food. Then, when everything was cooked and ready, he and some of the rabbits carried the plates out to the tables. Soon everybody was served and Philip sat down next to Mr Edgar and Mrs Badger to eat his own food. It was absolutely delicious and he couldn't resist having seconds.

Then, when everybody was full up with all the good food, Mr Edgar tapped his knife on the table and got up to speak.

'My dear friends, this is a very special party, a double party – a "Hello" and a "Goodbye" party rolled into one. We're saying "Hello and Welcome Back" to our three young heroes, but it's also a "Goodbye and Good Luck" party because tomorrow young Philip and I are going to leave you for a while.'

Mr Edgar paused as everybody looked at each other in surprise.

'Now, I don't know how long we will be gone but it doesn't really matter because I've got another important piece of news for you. Baby B and Nick, can you come here, please?'

Baby B and Nick ran to Mr Edgar and he lifted them on to the table so that everyone could see them. They stood there, shyly holding paws, as Mr Edgar went on.

'I know that all of you will be as pleased as I am to hear that these two young scamps behaved so bravely while they were off on their dangerous mission that they have learned how to think-talk.'

There was a gasp of delight and then all the animals began clapping and cheering and stamping their feet. Baby B and Nick looked down at the table and blushed so much that the tips of their noses turned bright pink.

'So,' said Mr Edgar, when the noise finally stopped, 'while we are away, Philip and I will be able to keep in touch with you through Baby B and Nick. Now, that's enough serious chin-wagging for this evening – we're supposed to be having fun. And, my hat, since it's a double party, let's make sure we have twice as much fun. So, come on, everybody, let's start with a dance.'

It was a smashing party. They sang and danced and told stories and jokes, and the castle rang with music and laughter and chatter until late into the night. Then, tired but happy, they all went off to bed.

Mrs Badger had made up a bed for Philip in Baby B's room and they both undressed quickly and blew out the candle. Philip lay for a while looking out of the window at the millions of bright stars twinkling in the sky. He thought about what Mr Edgar had said about how the earth was whizzing through space and yet it didn't seem as if it was moving at all.

It was strange about Mr Edgar. Philip had always known that the old beaver could do magic and unusual things, but he had never realized that it was much more important than that. All this time Mr Edgar had been working to help the whole world and yet he had never boasted about it or made himself look important. The very opposite, in fact – he was always talking about himself as 'the old duffer' and laughing at himself. And as

Philip thought about this he knew that it was another thing that he had started to learn.

From across the room, Baby B yawned and began singing the song softly:

Run to Beaver Towers, run to Beaver Towers.
Through the wind and through the showers,
Past the trees and past the flowers.
It took us hours and hours
But we're back at Beaver Towers.

'I'm glad we is back here, Flipip,' Baby B said sleepily.

'So am I,' Philip said.

'Night, Flipip.'

'Night, Baby B.'

A few minutes later, they were both asleep. Beneath them the earth moved on, whizzing silently through space and spinning them gently towards morning and a new day.

Choosing a brilliant book
can be a tricky business...
but not any more

www.puffin.co.uk

The best selection of books at your fingertips

So get clicking!

Searching the site is easy – you'll find what you're looking for at the click of a mouse, from great authors to brilliant books and more!

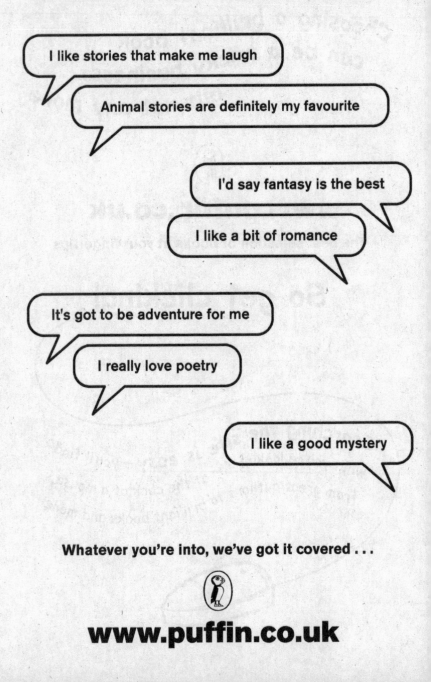

hotnews@puffin

Hot off the press!

You'll find all the latest exclusive Puffin news here

Where's it happening?

Check out our author tours and events programme

Best-sellers

What's hot and what's not? Find out in our charts

E-mail updates

Sign up to receive all the latest news
straight to your e-mail box

Links to the coolest sites

Get connected to all the best author web sites

Book of the Month

Check out our recommended reads

www.puffin.co.uk

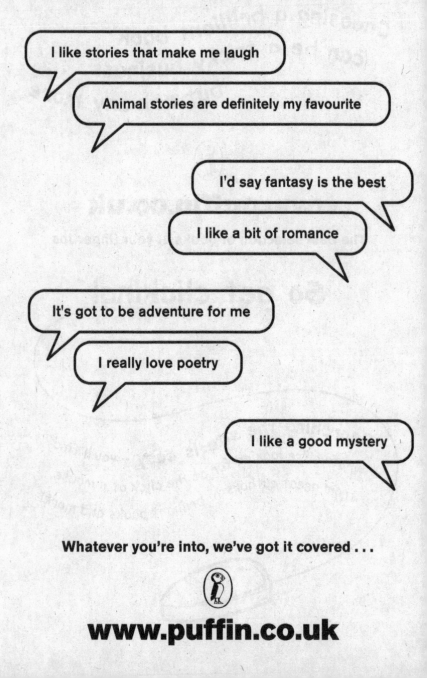

www.puffin.co.uk.www.puffin.co.uk.www.puffin.co.uk
bookinfo.competitions.news.games.sneakpreviews
www.puffin.co.uk.www.puffin.co.uk.www.puffin.co.uk
adventure.bestsellers.fun.coollinks.freestuff
www.puffin.co.uk.www.puffin.co.uk.www.puffin.co.uk
explore.yourshout.awards.toptips.authorinfo
www.puffin.co.uk.www.puffin.co.uk.www.puffin.co.uk
greatbooks.greatbooks.greatbooks.greatbooks
www.puffin.co.uk.www.puffin.co.uk.www.puffin.co.uk
reviews.poems.jokes.authorevents.audioclips
www.puffin.co.uk.www.puffin.co.uk.www.puffin.co.uk
interviews.e-mailupdates.bookinfo.competitions.news

www.puffin.co.uk

games.sneakpreviews.adventure.bestsellers.fun
www.puffin.co.uk.www.puffin.co.uk.www.puffin.co.uk
bookinfo.competitions.news.games.sneakpreviews
www.puffin.co.uk.www.puffin.co.uk.www.puffin.co.uk
adventure.bestsellers.fun.coollinks.freestuff
www.puffin.co.uk.www.puffin.co.uk.www.puffin.co.uk
explore.yourshout.awards.toptips.authorinfo
www.puffin.co.uk.www.puffin.co.uk.www.puffin.co.uk
greatbooks.greatbooks.greatbooks.greatbooks
www.puffin.co.uk.www.puffin.co.uk.www.puffin.co.uk
reviews.poems.jokes.authorevents.audioclips
www.puffin.co.uk.www.puffin.co.uk.www.puffin.co.uk